Remains to be Seen

The remains—those of a lecherous Armenian whom he had met precisely once in unforgettable circumstances—were to be seen in the back of Bernard Davis's car, where they had been dumped when Bernard left it parked in a London street on one of his trips to the capital to dispose of the jewels his father so mysteriously produced from time to time.

Of course his father, head of the family undertaking firm of Fitch, Davis & Sons in Scunthorpe, had escaped from Russia after the Revolution with the title of Prince Davydov, but that hardly explained why Soviet agents should be interested in him now, especially as the tyrannical old patriarch was dying. But when Bernard realized he was being followed and that there was a positively international concentration of interest in the Davis–Davydov family, it was as obvious as glad rags at a funeral that there had to be something else at stake.

There was—but by the time Bernard learnt that his father had left Russia with something more potent than a title, the precious object, of interest to four Intelligence services, had gone almost beyond recall. Luckily Bernard, the only non-undertaker in the family, outwitted all comers and ensured it a safe resting-place, not to mention disposing of the Armenian's remains.

by the same author

Black Comedies
THE FIVE MILLION DOLLAR PRINCE
A VIRGIN ON THE ROCKS
THE MAN WHO BROKE THE BANK AT MONTE CARLO
X MARKS THE SPOT
THE MAN IN THE SOPWITH CAMEL

Suspense Thrillers
FESTIVAL!
VILLA ON THE SHORE
THE BLACK LOOK
FLOWERS FOR A DEAD WITCH
VANISHING ACT
THE SOUNDLESS SCREAM
WALK SOFTLY, IN FEAR

MICHAEL BUTTERWORTH

Remains to be Seen

A Title in
THE DIAMOND JUBILEE COLLECTION

COLLINS, 8 GRAFTON STREET, LONDON W1

William Collins Sons & Co. Ltd
London · Glasgow · Sydney · Auckland
Toronto · Johannesburg

First published 1976
Reprinted in this Diamond Jubilee edition 1990
© Michael Butterworth 1976

ISBN 0 00 231229 8

Printed in Great Britain by
William Collins Sons & Co. Ltd, Glasgow

For Adrian Vincent

SCUNTHORPE, Humberside (formerly Lincolnshire). Pop. 69,330. Early closing Wednesday. Market Days, Monday to Saturday. 160 miles London. Municipal Offices: Ashby Road, Scunthorpe. Brigg & Scunthorpe Parliamentary division. Member (1974) Mr J. Ellis (Lab. 6,742 maj.) Industries: iron and steel; building and roadmaking materials; benzole and tar distillation; light engineering; footwear and clothing.

(reproduced by kind permission of
the *Eastern England Gazetteer*)

CHAPTER I

The Monday in June 1974 that Thomas J. Dade, supervisor of the Tsarist Russia (Residuals) Section, entered his office building was superficially like every other June day. Just as the building was similar to all the others in the block; and the blocks all alike in that particular part of Washington which – it has to be said – has gone downhill badly, socially, economically, ethnically since the TR(R) section was first set up, in the scary aftermath of the Bolshevik Revolution, under the Woodrow Wilson administration.

Dade took the elevator to the third floor, dying a little with each shudder of the ancient rig. At the door of his office, he paused – as he had paused every time in the twenty-five years since he had been with the section, first as assistant supervisor then as chief – and lightly tapped the Morse Code for the letters T and R upon the frosted glass door that bore the legend: *Mid-Eastern Holdings, Inc. – Private.*

Then he opened the door, which was unlocked.

His assistant supervisor, sole colleague, sole assistant, did not look up from his desk. DeSoto was working on his tax return, which kept him amused for the six months of the year that he didn't go fishing. DeSoto stood convinced on two premises: one, that there was an infallible roulette system waiting to be discovered; two, that the fiscal system of the United States was similarly vulnerable to the sly blandishments of a smart operator.

DeSoto was twenty-five years of age and, like his chief, unmarried.

'Coffee's just boiled,' he announced.

'Any mail?' enquired Dade, as he always did.

There were brochures and other hand-outs of a similar, importunate nature. How they all got hold of the name and address was a wonder, for Mid-Eastern Holdings were not listed in the phone book and sent out no communications under that styling.

'Nothing from Department?' asked Dade wistfully.

'We had the Christmas card in December,' said DeSoto. 'The annual request for an inventory of office furniture, paper clips, etcetera, etcetera, will hopefully arrive around the end of August, or we are both going to feel very miffed. Was it always like this?'

Dade poured himself a coffee; added a couple of calorie-free sweetening tablets.

'It was in around 'fifty,' he said. 'Or maybe 'fify-five, that Twentieth Century-Fox put out this *Anastasia* movie with Bergman and Brynner. All through that period of time when the movie was showing, I would say that the Department's interest in this section was increased in every regard. Every day brought rafts of enquiries about this and that concerning Tsarist Residuals. Like, is this Anderssen broad really the Grand Duchess Anastasia after all? And should we not really thoroughly check out Mike Romanoff, just in case? I'm telling you, Merv, the attitude with regard to this section took an upward turn on account of the *Anastasia* movie situation. And you know how *attitude* extends in this city.'

'I know absolutely, Tom.'

'It extends far beyond the Department, far beyond Government.'

'I would totally agree.'

'It extends to the social situation. This thing, Merv – this *attitude* thing – I would say extends in this city as far as the very cab-drivers, the hookers, the bartenders, the maitre-d's in the goddamned restaurants. Am I overstating, Merv?'

'Not from where I'm sitting, Tom. No, sir.'

'I swear before God, Merv, that the *Anastasia* movie temporarily changed the attitude thing in this city to the section that, while the situation obtained, your predecessor and I were enjoying better service in at least a couple areas. He was being propositioned by a better style hooker, while I was getting more prestigious tables in all the restaurants. Do you dig?'

'Absolutely, Tom. I'm following your line of reasoning perfectly.'

Dade drained his coffee-cup and stared into the dregs with the wary air of an oft-disappointed augur reading entrails.

'They're going to close down the section,' he said. 'It has to come. There isn't a residual around the place that would raise a flicker of interest from the Department. Hell, most of the old-timers are dead, and their descendants have been absorbed into whatever local social situation. Merv, Tsarist Grand Dukes don't play commissionaire outside movie theatres like they did in the 'twenties and 'thirties – meantime plotting to overthrow the Soviets by force.' He shook his head sadly. 'I'm so close to my pension that it scarcely matters, but I weep for you, Merv, I surely do.'

'Hell, I can make a fresh start in another section!' cried DeSoto stoutly.

His superior shook his head. 'I want to post you on the

situation, Merv,' he said. 'In the three years you've been with me – three great, hard-working years, mind; not your fault the breaks didn't come along – the other guys, your contemporaries, have been having a ball, careerwise.' He leaned forward and tapped the younger man on the knee. 'Figure for yourself how they must be making out in Urban Guerrila Watch, or Student Unrest – not to speak of the manifest opportunities promotionwise enjoyed by the guys in Pornography and Fringe Religions. You've got a long ways to pull up, Merv, and those guys aren't going to give you a free ride. No, sir. Not on your background with dear old TR(R).'

The distant wail of a police siren faded off downtown. DeSoto was drawing sullen spirals on his tax calculations.

'It burns my tail,' he growled, 'that we can't raise couple breaks from the files, or someplace. Something really hot. An abortive rising against the Soviets, for instance. Put the section on the map. Just to see me through my transfer to another section, and you move out to retirement in a blaze of glory, Tom.'

Dade stared hard at his assistant. 'We smell out a rising,' he said slowly, 'that could mean a special appropriation. New staff. New furniture. Maybe a new office. It could lead to the *Anastasia* movie syndrome again, only bigger. But we don't have an anti-Soviet rising on file at this present time, Merv. Nor any similar situation.'

DeSoto held his superior's gaze. 'Do we not?' he murmured with mock innocence.

Midnight found them, shirtsleeved and sitting on the office floor, with the contents of the filing cabinets strewn around in piles relating to age, activities, backgrounds, and so forth. They had also concocted a few sketch-scenarios.

At midnight, DeSoto came up with a name . . .

'Davydov, Vladimir!'

'Aristocrat?' demanded Dade. 'Titled? A regular *boyar*?'

'Prince Vladimir Davydov,' confirmed the other. 'Aged – ah – that'll be seventy-six. Large family. Three kids. Ah – seven grandchildren. Two great-grandchildren. Call it a dynasty.'

'Origin?'

'Mmmm – Kiev. The Ukraine. Scenario B.'

'Scenario B,' said Dade crushingly, 'I favour least of all! We are not going to get screwed around with that thing, not if anything else offers. Where is this Davydov now resident?'

'Umm – Scunthorpe.'

'Scunthorpe?'

'Scunthorpe, England.'

Dade drew in a lungful of cigarette smoke and exhaled it, meanwhile staring thoughtfully at the ceiling.

'All place names,' he said presently, 'have an emotional pitch – a timbre, if you know what I mean – to their very sound. Samarkand, for instance, now that is emotively a very brave and splendid sound. So is – ah – Trebizond. In the emotive area, however, I find Scunthorpe is right at the opposite end of the scale from the two examples I have mentioned. It is to me totally bathetic. Am I overstating?'

'No. Right!' DeSoto assured him. 'But, the name aside, Davydov has a lot of pluses going for him.'

'To name but three?'

'One, he's utterly clean,' said DeSoto, scanning the

file. 'Never stuck his nose into politics. Clean as a whistle. One day in nineteen-nineteen, March of that year, we have this twenty-one-year-old ensign of the Imperial Guards fleeing northwards from the Red Army forces that have entered Kiev. He has an automobile and his personal baggage, when he runs into a British army patrol outside Murmansk. Next he is transferred to England by Royal Navy destroyer. Port of entry, Kingston-upon-Hull. In nearby Scunthorpe, Ensign Prince Vladimir Ilich Davydov of the Imperial Guards later changes his name to Vernon Davis and enters into business as partner in a firm of morticians.'

'Morticians, you say?'

'More correctly, undertakers,' replied DeSoto. 'In Britain they call them undertakers or funeral directors.'

'A Ukrainian prince of the nobility,' mused Dade. 'A *boyar* turned provincial undertaker. And from Kiev.'

'Our people have gotten plenty information on him,' said DeSoto. 'Among the body of fact in our possession is a deposition made by the prince to the British Home Office, testifying that his family palace outside the city was burned down during the Reds' advance and all his people killed. Here's something else: although the prince married an Englishwoman, and two of his three sons did likewise, the grandchildren all bear Russian names. And here's a clincher: the wife of number one son is currently taking instruction in the Russian language. How does Scenario B grab you now?'

Dade blew a smoke ring.

'Hang it on me for size, Merv,' he said. 'Recite it to me, right through. If it rings true, that scenario goes to the Department first thing tomorrow. If they buy it, we could be in business. Big business.'

CHAPTER II

The east wind, fresh from the Urals, that scoured the Humber estuary and Scunthorpe High Street, rattled the window-frame of Bernard Davis's living-room and caused his gas fire to pop and flare.

Bernard shivered in the thin silk dressing-gown that he wore over two sweaters. It was a totally useless robe that he had bought on his last trip to London because it called to his mind the sort of drooping-eyed decadence that he always associated with Paris of the early thirties, absinthe, the nude paintings of Jean-Gabriel Doumergue, and the cabaret work of the late Sir Noël Coward. Shivering, he re-addressed himself to his task.

Distant yet omnipresent music of airy pipes,
Wispy faerie imaginings . . .

He considered the lines in his notebook, silver propelling-pencil poised over the page, for a few moments; then, with his neat and elegant italic script, he replaced 'pipes' with 'flutes'. He repeated the lines over to himself several times, and nodded with satisfaction. That done, he laid the notebook carefully in a drawer of his desk, retracted the lead of his pencil and placed it in a grooved receptacle on the cut-glass ink-well. A glance at his watch told him it was three-thirty: time to go.

Bernard Davis – self-declared poet and man of letters – occupied a four-roomed self-contained flat over Monica's Boutique in the High Street, with a private entrance next to the shop door; a circumstance that brought his comings and goings constantly to the watchful eye of Monica, a small young woman with a brisk manner and an admirable *poitrine*, of whom Bernard stood in some dread, because of her habit of responding to the simplest observations on his part – such as, 'Nice weather for the time of the year,' or 'Would you please give a message to the milkman?" – by coming very close to him and looking up with eyelashes a-flutter, bosoms heaving, and a moistening of candy-pink lips with a very pointed tongue. Bernard, who saw a sinister coquetry in all women who did not treat him with the dismissiveness to which he had long grown accustomed, was somewhat mistaken in his summation of Monica's character; her briskness, insistence on propinquity, and rapid aspiration were caused by nerves, a slight deafness, and asthma respectively. Nevertheless, she secretly found Bernard attractive : the moistening of the lips – which, as she had learned from her favourite magazine, is what fashion models do before facing the lens – and the eyelash fluttering, that was all for him.

She was close by her shop door, rearranging a revolving display of suavely-packaged brassières, when he came out of his door and into the street. Though he strained to avert his gaze, sheer timidity dragged his eyes to acknowledge hers. She nodded and silently mouthed 'Good afternoon,' fluttering her eyes, and then remembered to moisten her lips.

Bernard's nicely-kept 1958 Aston Martin saloon lolled sleekly in a nearby back street, outside the Cathay Flower Take-Away Chinese Restaurant. Bland Oriental faces glanced up from their tasks and grinned through the plate-glass windows of the kitchen at Bernard as he slid into the driving-seat and drove away.

It was only three blocks to Vicarage Gardens; scarcely

enough distance to take the Mark III through its gearbox and back, but he enjoyed the surge and withdrawal of power, which he equated to poetry. There were two other cars parked outside his father's house, which meant he was the last to arrive. His blue sports car looked out of place beside his brothers' staid vehicles of funereal black; a peacock among ravens. The word 'blue' conjured up an association. He paused on the step, took out a small notebook and pencil that he always carried, and scribbled:

Borne on these wondrous, elf-lit
Blue and gold-hued . . .

The door was suddenly opened by his father's housekeeper Minna Hodge, who had seen him enter the gate and walk up the path. He gave a start and snapped his notebook shut. Minna, a local woman, had taken over the housekeeping duties – and others of a more personal nature – on the death of Bernard's mother five years previously. Before then, she had been maid-of-all-work, and rigorously kept in her place. She heartily detested Bernard, and the sentiment was returned.

'You're late!' she snapped. 'They're all standin' around and waitin' to go up.'

He ignored the rebuke and pocketed the notebook. The piece was going quite nicely, he thought. Very *fin-de-siècle*. Debussy would have wished to set it to music. The family was gathered in the large, oak-panelled hall at the foot of the stairs. He assembled a bland mask as protection against his two brothers' and their wives' and children's and children's children's hostile glances.

'Hello, all,' he said brightly. 'Sorry to keep you. How's Father, do you know?'

'The Prince,' said his sister-in-law Kitty, 'had another bad night. The sooner he's got this afternoon's ordeal over, the better,' she added disapprovingly.

'We would have gone up already,' said Kitty's husband, the elder brother Alec, 'but we are thirteen.'

Alec, an undertaker, was surely in a better situation than most to know that Death is singularly uninfluenced in his activities by lucky portents, whether of good or ill, thought Bernard. But, then, Alec was not a very good, nor a very willing, undertaker, though he had certainly applied himself to the task of making the firm more competitive in a very tough market; alone of all the local operators, Fitch, Davis & Sons offered an attractive discount on embalmment – which goes to show that it pays to shop around.

'We'd better go along up, then,' said Maureen, the other sister-in-law, who felt that Alec and Kitty were, as usual, taking charge of everything. She gave her husband a nudge from behind. 'Lead the way, James!'

But years of taking second place to his elder brother had conditioned docile James against any such mischievous attempt at usurpation. With a delicate cough, such as those of their discipline employ to attract each other's attention at the graveside or during tense moments in the crematory chapel, he caught Alec's eye and directed it towards the stairs. Gravely acknowledging his brother's gesture with a slight inclination of his head, Alec offered his arm to Kitty and they led the way; followed by the obedient wake of their four daughters, Olga, Tatiana, Maria and Anastasia, who ranged in age from twenty-seven down to seventeen; with Olga carrying her baby girl Alexandra. James and his wife and family came after; leading from their unmarried son Alexis and his teenaged sisters Kira and Natasha – the latter carrying her infant son Sydney, whose paternity was currently the subject of an interesting correspondence – largely issuing from one direction – between the Davis's family solicitor and a young deck-hand of the Grimsby fishing fleet. Olga's husband was not present, being also of the sea-going persuasion. Bernard brought up the rear. Minna had already gone on ahead, to warn her master of his offspring's imminent arrival.

Prince Vladimir Ilich Davydov, yclept Vernon Davis, lay propped up against a great bolster on his marriage bed in the largest of the front bedrooms. The very length and leanness of the sprawled legs under the sheets gave an impression of tallness, even in the reclining position. This was accentuated by the thinness of the long neck that rose – wattled like the neck of a tortoise – from wide and exceedingly bony shoulders that were only lightly veiled by the open collar of a striped woollen nightshirt. The head was striking: the snowy hair close-cropped; a Tartar cast to the sloping eyes and high cheekbones; a sabre scar on the left cheek. A bony hand transferred a cigarette to the thin mouth, and it was admitted with a flash of stainless steel teeth. The patriarch blew out a cloud of smoke.

'All right then – where's t'bloody tea?'

Fifty-odd years' wear had fashioned the old Russian's accent into the lingua franca, which, Scunthorpe standing as it does at the watershed of the North Midlands, Yorkshire and Lincolnshire, partakes a little of each dialect. Obedient to her master's demand, Minna busied herself at the steaming brass samovar on the table by the curtained window; filling little glasses with the pale-coloured liquid and passing them to Anastasia and Kira, to hand to the others.

'I hope we see you in better health, Prince,' said Kitty

tremulously, stooping over to kiss one large knobbly paw that lay upon the sheet.

The patriarch ignored her.

'How's t'order book?' he demanded of his eldest son. 'This bloody east wind should be knocking 'em off the perch in their dozens.' He gave a bronchial cough of great textural complexity. 'If it doesn't give over bloody soon, it'll have me under the sod and all!'

'Plenty of business in hand, Father,' Alec assured him. 'And we're picking up our fair share of the seasonal increase, never fear.'

The old man's eyes flashed contemptuously to one and the other of his two black-garbed elder sons. 'You're not letting t'east wind keep you sitting on your bloody arses in t'office,' he growled. 'One or t'other of you's following every box, like I've always told you?'

Alec and James exchanged uneasy glances, and Bernard smiled to himself. Given the sort of weather one had been experiencing during the last four weeks, he could not imagine either of his brothers following a client's coffin either to cemetery or crematory chapel – not while they could provide themselves with the comforting alternatives of sales graphs, viability diagrams and the like, to play with. And yet the old man had always driven home to them the cardinal rule for a successful funeral director (learned from old Edmund Fitch, his late partner and mentor), which was that every funeral above the poverty line should be graced by the presence of one of the named directors: top hat in hand, head bowed, gathering the appreciation of the bereaved ('Mister Vernon Davis himself was following') and the certainty of repeat orders.

'One or the other of us puts in an attendance whenever possible, Father,' lied Alec.

The patriarch stabbed a bony forefinger at his eldest son.

'Ted Fitch always said to me, he said: "You'll never make a funeral director unless you get up off your arse and get behind that box! Top hat in your hand! Head bowed, and a sober and righteous look on your bloody face!" That was old Ted Fitch's motto – and he put whole families away, from grandads to babies!'

Alec and James made suitable appreciative noises. Little Sydney began to wail, and the old man cast a loathing glance in the direction of that innocent fruit of passion. He was already beginning to be tired and bored.

'Lay you down and get a bit of sleep,' said Minna Hodge, easing the bolster behind her master's head. He sank back, unresisting, with a curse.

'Goodbye, Father,' said Alec. 'We'll all come and see you again before Christmas.'

'I'll tell you when to come again,' snarled the patriarch. 'And don't show your bloody faces before!'

'It's been marvellous to find you in such good spirits, Prince,' declared Kitty. And she would have kissed his hand again, had not the old man seen it coming, and forestalled the move by slipping it hastily under the sheet and baring his stainless steel fangs at his daughter-in-law.

'Come, all,' said Alec. 'Say goodbye to Grandfather, all you children, and let's be gone. Grandfather's tired.'

The patriarch had closed his eyes. Without opening them, he growled: 'Bernard, you'll stay behind. I've got something to talk to you about.'

'I'm sure Bernard doesn't want to bother you . . .' began Alec.

The freezing eyes blazed upon the eldest son.

'Shut your bloody gob and get out!'

There was a hasty and general withdrawal from the bedroom. Kitty flashed a resentful glance at Bernard as he stood meekly holding the door for her. Minna Hodge was the last to leave.

'Sit down where I can see you,' snapped the old man. 'Christ, it's a bloody relief to be shut of that lot. That cow of Alec's! She gives me t'bellyache.'

'Yes, Father,' said Bernard. He wondered what the old man would have said if he knew that it was Kitty's intention that they all revived the old name and titles after he'd gone; and that she was learning Russian at the Tech.

'She's bloody crazy,' growled the patriarch. 'Give me a cigarette and pass me that cigar-box from the table.'

Bernard did as he was told.

'Now light me. Careful, you clumsy bugger! Do you want to burn me to death?'

'Sorry, Father.'

'Now go and lock t'door.'

This he did also.

'I want you to take a trip to London again,' said his father. 'To Hatton Garden.'

'All right, Father,' replied the other. 'What sort of piece is it this time?'

The patriarch's huge hands took the cigar-box, raised the lid and rummaged among tissue paper that lay within. With surprising delicacy, a winking source of white light was presented to Bernard between a bony finger and thumb. He took it and weighed it in his hand.

'You've picked up a thing or two throughout the years, daft as you are,' said his father. 'How much do you reckon for that?'

'This diamond?' said Bernard. 'Oh, I should think I can find a buyer – ready cash and no questions asked, as usual – for, say, five to eight thousand. Of course, on the open market I could get . . .'

'Give over about t'open market, you daft sod!' snarled his father. 'You know better than that. If t'bloody Bolsheviks could get their hands on that lot, we'd all end up like the Romanoffs, with daylight through our heads!'

'How much more of the stuff is there, Father?'

'Plenty!'

'Well,' persisted Bernard, greatly daring, 'I've been handling the pieces – taking them up to Hatton Garden – ever since I left school at eighteen and you swore me to secrecy and told me about the deal. In the – um – twenty-four years since then, I've handled one or two pieces most years, and nothing less than five thousand quid a throw. That means that since around nineteen-fifty, something like a hundred and eighty thousand of untaxed liquidity has passed into the family coffers.'

'Hundred and sixty-five,' corrected his father with a savage, stainless steel grin. 'I don't keep any books, but I've got a good head for figures.'

'Useful little nest egg you brought over from the old country, Father. Is it really . . . ours?'

The Tartar eyes narrowed dangerously. Despite his forty-two years, Bernard suddenly felt unaccountably young and vulnerable – as on the occasions in his childhood when his father had beaten him almost to unconsciousness.

'What do you mean, *ours*?'

'I mean, is it Davydov treasure? Family heirlooms and all that? Ouch, Father . . . you're hurting me!'

One of the big hands was about his left forearm, bony finger-ends probing deeply, painfully, into muscle tissues. He caught the rasp of his father's smell – stale tobacco and old man smell – as he was pulled close.

'T'bloody Bolsheviks took everything they wanted,' hissed the terrifying old man. 'Money, gold, jewels, women – everything! What I brought over to England was mine. *Mine*, do you hear? *My* share of Holy Russia! And don't you ever forget that!'

'No, Father,' said Bernard placatingly, rubbing his bruised forearm when it was released.

'As to how much more,' continued the patriarch. 'Plenty! Enough to keep you buggers in loose change for ever more and then some. I haven't been greedy. That's why I've still got it. It bought me a partnership in Ted Fitch's business, paid for this house. Paid to educate you layabouts. Kept the whole family liquid. Oh, I could have bought a yacht. Homes in Bermuda and the South of France, hob-nobbed with the nobility of Europe. And where would we all have ended up? I'll tell you . . .' And the old man indicated his meaning by putting a forefinger to the side of his head and pulling an invisible trigger.

'I understand, Father,' said Bernard with a shudder. 'But tell me: are they *really* so interested in what one aristocrat managed to get out of Russia all those years ago?'

Again the Tartar eyes narrowed, and Bernard instinctively withdrew his arm from the scope of his father's grasp.

'I'm telling you,' said the former Prince Vladimir Ilich Davydov evenly, 'that t'bloody Bolsheviks would give a division of crack infantry, or a heavy cruiser, or free half a million political prisoners, for what I brought back from Kiev in nineteen-nineteen!'

Bernard had secreted the really remarkably fine-cut diamond in a silk handkerchief in his trouser pocket when Minna Hodge tapped on the door and called out that Mr Podolski had arrived.

'You can stay and have a word with old bugger,' the patriarch ordered Bernard.

Casimir Podolski was Polish. He had come to England after the fall of his own country in 1940. Himself from the Polish Ukraine, he had met Bernard's father in a professional capacity while arranging, as adjutant of a Polish bomber squadron, for Messrs Fitch, Davis & Sons to attend the obsequies of such of his dead fliers as were available for interment in the rich earth of the Humber estuary. Podolski was sixty-six now, and newly-retired from being a traveller in footwear. A bachelor, he lived round the corner from Vicarage Gardens, and kept a regular date to play chess with the old undertaker every Wednesday evening. He was the only person whom Bernard had ever known to receive the scantiest civility at the hands of his father. And the only person to whom the patriarch ever addressed a word of Russian.

'Good evening, my dear Vernon. Why, it is you, also here, my dear Bernard!' Podolski's accent had remained untainted by the lingua franca; he was all Pole, from the top of his sleek, well-barbered head to the uppers of his highly-polished boots, five feet one inch lower down.

'Sit down, Casim,' growled the patriarch. 'Not too early for a bloody drink, I don't suppose?' And when

Podolski inclined his head and smiled slyly: 'Pour him a large vodka, Minna. How're you keeping, you randy old sod?'

Bernard stole a glance at his watch and decided that, mindful of the hundred-and-sixty-mile drive to London that he faced on the morrow, he would take his leave in ten minutes or so. An early night beckoned, but before that he wanted to finish the short romantic poem he'd been working on all day, the *fin-de-siècle* thing.

Distant yet omnipresent music of airy flutes . . .

Wasn't the word 'omnipresent' perhaps a trifle – well, heavy-weight for a romantic fantasy? A bit of a four-square word, like 'parallelogram' and 'oxydization'? What was omnipresent in French? He'd have to look it up. The trouble with writing poetry was the trouble with most creative pursuits he'd attempted: the early stages were absurdly easy, but once one took a second step, one was out of one's depth; there seemed nothing between ankle-deep and over one's head. It had been the same with his novel-writing.

Podolski was asking him something . . .

'I'm sorry, Casim,' he said. 'I was daydreaming about poetry.'

'It was about that I was asking you, my dear Bernard,' said Podolski. 'How is poetry going?'

Suddenly it became very difficult to talk about. He supposed he liked Casimir Podolski – he'd known him for long enough – but there was always something about the Pole's pale, peeled-looking eyes that disconcerted. And the old-world Slavonic charm – that scarcely concealed a cynicism which was betrayed, anyhow, by the mobile lips under that hawk's beak of a nose. He supposed Casim regarded him – and with some justification – as a middle-aged dilettante with a contemptuous but well-off daddy who supported him as an artist because he believed him incapable of doing anything else.

He said: 'Surprisingly well at the moment. Of course, I'm only working in a very small scale. Evocative fragments, really.'

'That is interesting. When shall you be ready to publish book of your poems, my dear Bernard?'

'Oh, I'm not thinking that far ahead,' said Bernard. 'I haven't produced a very large body of work, and, of course, I throw a lot of stuff away.' He had the impression that the Pole was probing him – and with a thin edge of malice and mockery. It was at this moment that he received some support of a sarcastic nature from his sire.

'Bernard's not quite the bloody fool he looks,' sneered the patriarch. 'After twenty years of hard grind, he managed to get an article accepted by t'*Humberside Magazine*.'

'I read it,' said Podolski. 'I thought article was quite enchanting. About Scunthorpe Museum, was it not?'

Bernard made no comment. The magazine was little more than a glorified newsletter, and contributors were unpaid – as his father and Podolski very well knew.

(If only . . . if only he could break away! Go abroad! If only his father's support extended further than the short length of string that enabled him to drag him back at every whim . . .)

'Then there's his unpublished novels,' continued the old man. 'Two full-length novels, mark you. Oh yes, you might think he wasted all those years at Oxford, but you'd be wrong.'

There was a terrible silence. Bernard clenched his fists

till the fingernails almost bore into the palms.

(No wonder they had a bloody revolution! No wonder it lasted! No wonder they put up with bloody Stalin all those years! Anything must have seemed an improvement after your lot!)

'Well, I wish Bernard good luck with poetry,' said Podolski at length. 'So dedicated a *littérateur* should not have to wait for his reward from posterity.' And he chuckled at his little joke.

Bernard relaxed, and said: 'Well, I'd better be going. Enjoy your chess game. I'll call and see you on Monday when I get back, Father.'

'You are taking trip, Bernard?' asked the Pole.

'He's off to London tomorrow,' growled the patriarch.

'Bon voyage,' said Podolski, and he rose to his feet — all five feet, one inch of him, stiff as a ramrod — clicked his heels and shook hands with Bernard.

'Where are you staying in London?' demanded the patriarch.

'The usual place, Father,' replied Bernard. 'Goodbye, sir. See you on Monday.'

'Mind you don't lose the you-know-what,' growled the former Prince Davydov. 'Lose that, and don't bother to come back!'

Bernard smiled nervously and patted his trouser pocket, where lay the family's latest item of untaxed liquidity.

Monica was just shutting up shop when he arrived back at the flat. She turned from locking her door and gave him a fluttering smile.

'Ah . . .' began Bernard.

'Yes?' They had never got around to using each other's names.

'I'm going away for a few days tomorrow morning,' he said. 'To London. I wonder – would you please? . . .'

'Stop the milk till you get back?' she supplied. 'Of course. Much better than leaving a note on the door. Like offering an invitation to burglars, I always say.' She moistened her lips.

'Till Monday,' said Bernard. 'I'll be back about midday Monday.'

A car drew up at the kerb. A discreet toot of the horn, and the man at the wheel flipped his hand to Monica. Bernard supposed he must be her boy-friend; he looked rather old for her.

'I've got to go,' said Monica.

'Yes. Thank you for . . .'

'That's all right,' she said. She got half-way to the car, then she turned. 'Have a nice time in London,' she called out to him.

'Thank you.'

He watched the car drive away down High Street and turn left at the next corner. Its departure left him feeling unaccountably diminished.

The date was Wednesday, December 11th. About six months had passed since Thomas J. Dade and his assistant Mervin DeSoto had concocted their scenario on the former Prince Vladimir Ilich Davydov and his family. In those six months, the fortunes of the Tsarist Russia (Residuals) section had improved out of all recognition: Dade had been given extra staff and promoted from Supervisor to Director; the section, upgraded to a Directorate, had been shifted to a smart new block in the very shadow of Capitol Hill. And Dade and DeSoto were enjoying the kind of fringe benefits that fall to those upon whom the gods smile in the Seat of Western Democracy.

CHAPTER III

What Bernard referred to as his 'usual' hotel is a large and impersonal establishment in the Charing Cross area that caters mainly for visiting business people, tourists, and out-of-town folk generally. It is the sort of place to suit the requirements of a disparate clientele: conventioneering Japanese; elderly sightseeing Americans; panting wool men from the West Riding and their accommodating secretaries.

Bernard left his Aston Martin in a multi-storey car park and carried his valise to the hotel, stopping off for a pint of keg beer on the way. He also bought a bottle of whisky and a magazine. The notes of Big Ben were sounding midday over London's grimy rooftops when he let himself into a room with bath on the third floor.

A stiff whisky nerved him to turn to the advertising section of his magazine, where, from a selection of a round dozen, he chose a name and a telephone number. Fingers slippery with the sweat of anticipation, he picked up the telephone receiver and asked the hotel switchboard to give him the number.

He heard the dialling tones. His heartbeat quickened. His breathing grew shallow and swift.

The ringing stopped.

'Five nine three . . .' came a voice – a woman's voice – at the other end.

'Sorry-wrong-number!' croaked Bernard.

He slammed down the receiver, and met his reflection in the mirror opposite. His face wore the expression of a little boy caught stealing jam.

'Are you a man or a mouse?' he demanded aloud – and gave himself no answer.

After which, there did not seem much else to do but to go down to the hotel bar.

Of the several bars, Bernard usually favoured the most highly-priced, which went in for dim lighting and piped music of a vaguely South American persuasion; and it was to this he went, ordering a scotch on the rocks, and scooping a handful of peanuts into his mouth with simian expertise.

He would do his business in Hatton Garden this afternoon, he decided. Then, with the cash proceeds posted by registered mail to his father, he would be able to relax and enjoy himself. Relaxation was everything – or so he had always read and believed. Perhaps when sufficiently relaxed by a good lunch and several more of these excellent scotches – he took a deep pull at the chilled spirit and winced when an ice cube chinked against a sensitive incisor – he would dare to ring that number again and make known his specific wants to the young female (she *sounded* a young female) who had answered the phone. And this opened up a further field of speculation: Just how specific *did* one have to be in these transactions? How much was proposed by the purveyor, and how much left for the client to propose? He sincerely hoped that a little gentle beating around the bush was all that would be necessary on his part.

'What damned nonsense!'

Bernard gave a start. It was the man on the bar stool next to him who had exclaimed. The lowering of a copy of the *Courier* revealed his neighbour to be a large man in his mid-fifties, with a bucolic complexion and supplementary chins to the number of at least three. He wore a moustache of the sort that used to be called a 'Ronald Colman'; and both that and his wealth of crinkly hair possessed an intense and suspect blackness. Black also – and full of merriment – were the eyes that turned to meet Bernard's alarmed stare. Bernard mentally docketed him as a foreigner. A Levantine.

'So sorry, my dear fellow. Did I alarm you?' said the stranger. 'I was expleting about this latest pronouncement from one of the current idols of the young generation – a generation who, from their present interpretation of the current scene – are scarcely likely to survive to be old fogeys like you and me.' If a Levantine, then decidedly articulate.

'I haven't seen the newspapers today,' said Bernard apologetically. 'Er – what are they up to now?'

'A student leader,' said his new acquaintance, referring back to his newspaper, 'one Mr G. F. Passingham-Waller, who is currently performing the well-nigh impossible feat of reading for the Bar and at the same time acting as president of an advanced revolutionary party, has proposed that the People's Republic of China be invited to pour finance into British universities on such a scale as to – in Mr Passingham-Waller's happy phrases – "facilitate the selection, for university places, of candidates who qualify by reason of political and social experience rather than irrelevant academic achievements". Now, that's nice, isn't it? What next? you may well ask.'

'There's a lot of stupid guff written about students,' said Bernard. 'I blame a lot of it on the media: they latch on to a silly remark like that and blow it up out of all relevance. It's a great many years since I was an undergraduate, but I'm sure things can't have changed all that much. You get the Wild Men and the Champagne Charlies; but the majority of people really do work themselves into a state of near-mental breakdown.'

'Ah, you are a fellow 'varsity man!' cried his companion. 'But, of course, it is written all over you. Was it Oxford or Cambridge?'

'Oxford,' replied Bernard shortly.

'I was at the Sorbonne, and later at Zürich,' said the other. 'My father was a professor of biomathematics, and I have been a humble acolyte of that same discipline. My card, sir.' And he took from out of a black crocodile-skin wallet an engraved visiting-card and handed it to Bernard.

Mr Aram Garbisian
Import & Export   Theatrical Agent

'Garbisian,' said Bernard, for want of something else. 'Ah, yes.'

'I am of Armenian extraction,' explained the other.

'You've a very good command of English,' said Bernard lamely. It really did sound very patronizing.

'Not bad for a bloody wog,' said Garbisian.

'Oh, I didn't mean . . .'

'Of course not, my dear fellow!' The berry-black eyes were sparkling with mirth as he nudged Bernard in the ribs. 'But I've been in England long enough to know that wogs begin at Calais. Not that I would ascribe such illiberal sentiments to a graduate of one of the ancient 'varsities.'

'I didn't graduate,' admitted Bernard dully. 'I was ploughed. I'm one of those chaps with the joke degree: Failed BA (Oxon).'

'And confidentially,' murmured Garbisian leaning close

to him, 'confidentially, my dear Mr, er . . .'

'Davis. Bernard Davis.'

'Confidentially, my dear Mr Davis,' continued Garbisian, 'I never quite got the hang of biomathematics, and there's more bread in the Import and Export business.'

'If you don't mind my asking, Mr Garbisian,' asked Bernard. 'How do you tie in the Import and Export business with that of Theatrical Agent?'

Garbisian beamed at him. 'It is simply a matter of merchandising, my dear fellow,' he said. 'I import and export – mostly export – *artistes*.'

'Oh, I see,' said Bernard, who didn't.

The Armenian fished out his wallet again; produced from it a sheaf of postcard-sized photographs, which appeared to be of vaudeville performers. He riffled through them, and showed a panorama of stage smiles on heavily made-up faces; tinsel and feathers and a great deal of leg; and a certain amount of near-nudity. They were all young girls.

'There's no business like show business,' winked his new friend. 'Join me in another drink, my dear Mr Davis.'

At Garbisian's insistence, they lunched together in the hotel grill-room. This, after another three large scotches apiece, and to the accompaniment of one and a half bottles of Valpolicella with their rare-done steaks.

The Armenian's articulateness was unimpeded; Bernard was doing his best through a haze of alcohol.

Garbisian was leading off about the young generation again; Bernard was defending them, more from a desire to draw out his companion's refreshingly illiberal opinions than from any deeply-felt convictions one way or another.

'You have to grant, Garbisian,' he said, 'that the youth of today, in seeking new answers to the eternal questions, have come up with some pretty exciting results.'

'New answers!' snorted Garbisian. 'I tell you, my dear Davis, that youth provides no answers. Youth stands on a slight vantage-point of semi-ignorance, from which contemptible promontory he gazes – ignoring the lush valley of knowledge and experience between – to the distant, barren heights of blind speculation.'

'I wonder,' said Bernard muzzily, 'I wonder that you don't find your detestation of the young a tremendous obstacle in your dealings with the young lady artistes, in your import and export work.'

Garbisian gave a discreet belch, patted his great belly and winked.

'My young ladies,' he said, 'my artistes, by the time they reach my hands, my dear Davis, they have already progressed, *via* sundry Saturday morning dancing classes held in unspeakable provincial church halls, to working the Northern working men's club circuit. I can assure you that nothing instils in a young girl a proper sense of life's realities like taking off her knickers before a packed audience of inebriated North Country working men; just as there is nothing in the Great University of Life to compare with leading a choir of the opposite sex in a rendition of Rugby Football songs for inculcating modesty and sincerity in a maidenly breast. By the time they reach me, my dear Davis, they are sincere, cynical, and tame. In the phrase of the vulgar, they know which side of their bloody bread is buttered.'

Bernard laid aside his knife and fork and took a long draught of wine. In his limited experience, he had never before come across a man whose attitude to the opposite sex was informed by such breezy, careless confidence amounting almost to cool contempt. His own approach to women, which was largely conditioned by his relationship with his late mother and with his brothers' wives, could be likened to that of a rabbit to a stoat.

Through the vapours of grape and grain, it came to him that here was an acquaintance to be exploited, an attitude to be explored . . .

'I suppose, Garbisian . . .' he began.

'Call me Aram,' said the other. 'Do, please, my dear Bernard.'

'I suppose, Aram, that your relationship with these young lady artists, who are of a certain type, not to say social class; though I don't want to bring class into this discussion . . .'

Aram Garbisian raised his plump hand in a gesture of deprecation.

'We will not prevaricate,' he said cheerfully. 'They are all as common as muck. Proper little scrubbers.'

Bernard swallowed hard, and continued: 'I suppose your connection with these – er – girls sometimes includes . . . includes . . .'

Garbisian was helpful as ever. 'I tumble the lot,' he declared. 'Without any trouble at all. They expect it of me.'

'Simply because of their type and class. And because, as you have said, they have had their illusions dispelled in a hard school.'

Garbisian looked genuinely puzzled. 'You must be having me on, my dear Bernard,' he said. 'Surely, in your own wide experience, you must have discovered that, in matters of sexual morality, there is nothing to choose between the daughters of dustmen and the daughters of dukes. In matters sexual, they are all sisters under the skin – as are my cynical little scrubbers and Mr Passingham-Waller's starry-eyed supporters. Come now – has this not been your experience?'

Bernard's mind went back to a searing memory of his Oxford days, when, on the occasion of a commemoration ball, he had had his face slapped by a young woman named Felicity for no other reason than that he had been so emboldened by champagne as tentatively to suggest that she might like to accompany him on a week-end to Brighton, an offer that he had never made before – or since – to any female.

'Quite so – er – Aram,' he said. 'That has always been my experience.'

'After all, we are both *men*, my dear Bernard,' said Garbisian. 'We are not like these fellows whose approach to the fair sex is doomed from the start by reason of inhibitory factors such as upbringing, mother-fixation, inferiority consciousness, anxiety, halitosis, and so forth. We ride full at our fences.'

'Throwing our hearts over first, so that our horses will follow!' cried Bernard stoutly.

'Faint heart never won fair lady!'

'None but the brave deserve the fair!'

'*Encore de l'audace! Et toujours de l'audace!*'

'Well, I must be going,' said Bernard abruptly. 'Waiter! I'll sign the bill.'

'We will split the bill,' said Garbisian. 'This has been most pleasant, my dear fellow. I suppose, like me, you have business to attend to this afternoon?'

'I had intended to do a little job of selling this afternoon,' confessed Bernard with a tipsy smile. 'But it can wait till tomorrow morning. This afternoon I have an urge to ride full at a fence!'

The Armenian rolled his eyes heavenwards and kissed his fingertips. 'A delicious impulse, my dear Bernard. The lady is to be congratulated. We must meet for a pre-prandial drink in the bar at noon tomorrow, and you shall give me an account of your afternoon's amour.'

'It's a date, Aram,' laughed Bernard. And he swaggered out of the grill-room. Yes, by Jove! *Encore de l'audace! Et toujours de l'audace!* The chance meeting with Garbisian had solved the problem of a lifetime.

While he was able to admit to himself, with what was surely a refreshing candour, that he was more than slightly drunk, Bernard was smugly conscious of feeling supremely capable of coping with any situation which might present itself. In a crowded lift on the way up to the third floor, he grinned a pretty woman to pink-faced embarrassment; and all the occupants stared after him in fascination when he got out and weaved unsteadily down the corridor to his room. Finding the room took some time. Finding his way in was yet another problem – fortunately solved by a passing chambermaid with a master key.

The magazine lay open near the telephone where he had left it. He picked up the receiver and made his wants known with forceful brusqueness that was going to be a keynote of the new Bernard Davis. He was put through to his number almost immediately.

'Hello?' A man's voice.

'Now look here,' said Bernard. 'I'd like you to send around one of your young wenches this afternoon. To give me a massage, you know.'

('Young wenches' struck the right, horsey, no-nonsense,

ride-full-at-your-fences note.)

'Oh yes, sir. What time?'

'Mmm – let's see. Four o'clock.' It was now three-fifteen.

'Very good, sir. Four o'clock it is.'

'Someone young and pretty, mind!' He gave a deep-chested open-air sort of laugh. 'None of your tired old hacks.'

'Right you are, sir.'

'Good. Hey, wait a minute. Don't you need to know where I am?'

'Oh yes, sir. That's right. Where are you?'

Bernard told the man at the other end. When he put down the receiver, he found that his knees were shaking. He poured himself a large scotch.

By three forty-five, he had had a shower and was stalking the room, to and fro, in his dressing-gown. Four paces one way, and back another four paces. The simple mechanics of the movement induced in him a state of mild euphoria.

The new Bernard Davis was about to make his first conquest. It would be a picayune encounter, certainly, and hardly worthy to put on record; no complaisant daughter of a duke, she, his victim-to-be; merely a paid drab. (Which reminded him that the account of this afternoon's doings would have to be fancied up for Garbisian's benefit tomorrow. Why not translate her into a duke's daughter? Why not indeed?)

When there came a discreet tap upon his door, Bernard stiffened with shock and dropped his glass. It landed on the carpet without breaking, and splashed its dregs on his bare feet.

'Who – who is it?' he croaked.

The tap was repeated.

Walking up and down in a straight line had induced a sort of inverted vertigo: the curved path he had to take round the armchair to the door caused him to stumble and nearly fall. Arriving at his destination, he held himself upright by clinging to the doorknob with both hands.

'Who's there?' he asked, greatly dreading.

'I'm from the massage service,' came a cool, female voice. 'Don't you want to let me in?'

Bernard looked about him in panic. He had an impulse to dart into the bathroom and lock the door. But would he ever reach there?

'Aaaah . . .' he began.

'Hello. Yes? Can't you get the door open?' came the voice, now amused.

'There . . . there's been a mistake!' he blurted.

'You ordered a girl from the massage service, didn't you? To come to your hotel room at four o'clock?'

'Yes. But . . .'

'Well, I'm here.'

'Yes, but . . .'

'Have you changed your mind?'

'Well . . .'

'All right. But I'm afraid you'll still have to pay me. Can I come in?'

Bernard unlocked the door and opened it. She was tall. The top of her blonde head came to the level of his eyes. Her eyes were very large, blue and humorous. Her face had an out-of-doors, healthy look, like a Californian girl in an orange-juice advertisement, covered all over the tan with pale ginger freckles. Her lipstick was very red, her teeth very white.

'Hello,' she said, offering her hand. 'My name's Janice.'

'Bu-Bernard Davis,' he slurred. 'How do you do?'

She had on a black leather coat with an astrakhan collar, and she removed it and laid it on the back of the armchair; this left her in a white linen coat such as some dentists' receptionists wear; it did nothing to disguise the fact that she had an outstandingly remarkable figure and was wearing very little underneath. Bernard dropped his gaze and swayed back on his heels.

'Well, darling. What's it to be?' she asked him gently.

His racing mind darted for its accustomed bolthole of civility.

'Would – um – would you care for a drink?' he asked her.

'No, thank you, dear. And I don't think you need any more, do you?'

'I'm afraid,' confessed Bernard, 'that I am a little drunk.'

'Never mind,' she smiled. 'You'll enjoy it all the more.'

Her competent, strong hands took him by the shoulders and turned him round; unresistingly, he felt her unfasten the waistbelt of his dressing-gown and peel it off him. She gently guided him towards the bed. A playful push was all that was needed to prostrate him upon the soft eiderdown.

Strong fingers ploughing into the big muscles of his back. Bernard smiled into the pillow and let go of everything. That was the end of it, as far as he was concerned.

He opened one eye, and took in the weave of white bed linen. Memory returned by slow instalments: this was not the bedroom of his flat in Scunthorpe; this was London: it was not morning; it was some other time:

something had happened; and it was not simply that he had got drunk: another person was involved . . .

The girl!

He raised himself up, and winced at a spasm of pain that played like a lightning flash across his temple.

He was alone, and loosely covered by his dressing-gown, as if she had laid it over him before taking her departure. His watch was on the bedside-table, where he had left it after his shower, together with a handful of loose change; it was eight-thirty. Night's blackness through the crack in the curtained window showed that it was, indeed, still Thursday the twelfth. He had slept for – four and a half hours.

What about the girl? What was her name? – Janice!

Presumably, she had given him a purely symbolic massage, after he passed out, and had then left.

With or without her fee?

He rolled off the bed. The vertical position revealed with agonizing clarity that he had far from slept off the effects of his lunchtime debauch with Garbisian. Offering up a gentle curse to the Armenian, he delicately crossed over to the wardrobe, where his suit was draped on a hanger suspended from the doorknob. The wallet was in the breast pocket where he had left it: he thumbed the sheaf of notes inside; about twenty-five pounds was right – and his bank card and cheque book were still there. And his loose change. And his watch – given to him by Father: an expensive toy that told the time with four winking digits – was still there.

He checked his trousers, and knew on the instant that they had been moved: drunk or sober, his deeply-ingrained tidiness would never have permitted him to lay them over the bar in such a slovenly manner, without aligning the creases. And one of the pocket linings was half hanging out.

She had been through his suit. What else?

Three spare shirts and sets of socks, handkerchiefs and underclothing lay in the drawers of the dressing-table; together with a few odds and bobs like a pair of hairbrushes, a bottle of aspirin, a tin of throat lozenges, some dandruff lotion, the keys of the Aston.

The Aston!

Bernard was dressed in two minutes, and out of the hotel in five. An east wind blew down the long corridor of the Strand as he ducked up a side street in the direction of the multi-storey car park; the boisterous chill seemed to underline the urgency of his errand; sinking his chin more deeply into his overcoat collar, he broke into a steady trot.

The east wind followed him up the spiral steps to the second deck of the park, where it buffeted in and out of the open spaces; it almost snatched the door of the Aston from his hand when he swung it open and threw a leg inside, sinking back into the driver's seat.

Alone and shut in, he reached behind him, under the lowered flap that gives the rear seats of a Mark III Aston Martin the facility of an estate car, and probed under the corner of the fitted carpet of the floor. His hand came up with the diamond in its palm, a single pinpoint of reflected light burning whitely from the heart of the stone.

He knew that he never could have rested the night without checking on the gem.

The girl Janice had been through his belongings. The things in the drawers had been left tidy; but not quite Bernard Davis tidy.

A would-be pilferer? Then why had she not taken money from his wallet? Would he ring the massage service (which boasted a round-the-clock service) and complain? No, he knew he would never dare.

Then he had the uneasy thought – instantly suppressed – that the Bolsheviks might somehow have got wind of his errand. Quite ridiculous.

He returned the diamond to its hiding-place, locked up, and went back to the hotel – to bed.

CHAPTER IV

Friday the Thirteenth dawned early for Bernard Davis, when the excesses of the previous day woke him in the small hours and exacted harsh retribution. Afterwards, he sat on the edge of the bath and thought back gloomily to the brief but promising career of the new Bernard Davis. It was in this chancy position that he slept, in uneasy snatches, till wintry daylight seeped in through the frosted windows. He breakfasted on a cup of black coffee, and left the hotel immediately after. The clocks were striking nine-thirty as he parked the Aston at a meter just off Hatton Garden. The sky was heavily overcast and promising imminent rain.

HAMMET & SCRUBY
Dealers in Precious Stones

The entrance was up two steps and through a glass-fronted door, which had been repainted since his last visit. The act of opening it produced a loud clang, and caused the man behind the reception counter to look up from a ledger. Bernard knew him to be Hammet: he was fifty-ish, balding, and complexioned like a piece of old parchment. He peered at his visitor suspiciously, over rimless half-glasses.

'Yes?'

'We've done business before, Mr Hammet,' said Bernard, by way of laying the ground bait. 'Last March I sold you a couple of very fine rubies around two carats each. Nice pigeon's-blood colour. Remember?'

'I do a lot of business,' muttered the other. 'Buying and selling all the time. I can't remember everybody. What name?'

'Danby,' replied Bernard smoothly. One could scarcely have got a worse reception, he thought, if one had come in with a begging bowl – or a pistol. 'I've got a nice little brilliant-cut diamond for you today. Going for immediate cash. I've got to be in Rome this evening.'

'Let's have a look at it, then,' said Hammet sullenly.

Bernard unzipped the crocodile-skin briefcase that he carried, and took out the balled-up silk handkerchief, from which he produced the diamond and placed it in the centre of a black rectangle of velvet that lay on the counter, in such a way that Hammet was presented with the table, or flattened top, of the gem and its surrounding thirty-two facets.

'Nice little stone,' said Bernard. 'Flawless and well-coloured. Marvellous brilliance and fire, don't you think?'

'What's your price?' growled Hammet, eyeing the glittering bauble with contempt.

'It's about eight carats,' replied Bernard, tugging at his lip reflectively. 'Shall we say – ten thousand?'

The dealer sucked in a horrified gust of breath and closed his eyes with sudden pain. The pain abated, he picked up the gem and revolved it in his fingers. Then, lifting his spectacles, he stuck a magnifying glass in an eye and had a close-up. What he saw there made him suck in another mouthful of air.

'I think you're on a forty per cent mark-up with this diamond,' he pronounced glumly.

'Make me an offer,' retorted Bernard.

'I'll just get the weight,' said Hammet.

'Do that, Mr Hammet,' said Bernard. And when the other made to move in the direction of a door at the back of the counter, he added evenly, 'I'd rather you weighed it in my presence, if you don't mind. No offence intended.'

The dealer cast him a sharp look that was compounded of affront and respect in fairly equal proportions. Bernard had never been robbed during any of his transactions, but his father told of a time when a ruby had suffered the unaccountable loss of a quarter-carat while being weighed in another room – in other words, the dealer had worked a switch.

Hammet produced a balance scale, and pronounced Bernard's diamond to weigh 8·29 carats.

'I couldn't go beyond six grand for this diamond,' he said.

'It's a good thing I don't believe what they say in the papers about diamonds having appreciated by between sixty and a hundred per cent this year,' jested Bernard.

'Never believe what you read in the papers,' said Hammet.

Bernard picked up his diamond and wrapped it carefully in the handkerchief again. 'I'll call by again next time I'm in London,' he said quietly. 'Might have another nice pigeon's-blood ruby for you.'

Hammet's eyes had taken on a hunted look. 'You did

say immediate cash, didn't you?' he muttered.

'That's right,' said Bernard. 'I like to keep my transactions . . . you know . . . liquid.'

'I might go to seven.'

'Call it eight.'

'Seven and a half.'

'Done.'

Hammet took the diamond from the handkerchief, gave it a careful squint – to make sure that his client had not worked a switch! – and placed the gem in full view on an office desk in the middle of the room. He then went out the door at the back, and returned within a few minutes, carrying a thick wad of banknotes.

'Seven and a half grand in twenties,' he said. 'You'd better count them.'

'I'll do that, Mr Hammet,' said Bernard.

Riffling through the banknotes, he was aware of the dealer's eyes on him, sizing him up.

'You get hold of some nice gems, Mr – er – '

'Danby.'

'You get some nice merchandise, Mr Danby,' said the other. 'Those two rubies, for instance. They were so well matched, I'd think they both came out of a single setting. Am I right?'

'They might have been paired,' said Bernard, 'but I wouldn't know. We only handle unmounted gems.'

'I seem to remember that you mostly specialize in diamonds and rubies,' said Hammet. 'Am I right?'

'We handle anything,' replied Bernard firmly. 'Right across the board. Well, that seems to be okay, Mr Hammet. I'll say adieu. Nice to do business with you.'

'Call again, Mr Danby,' said the other with a wintry approximation to a smile, offering his hand. 'It's nice to see some real quality merchandise.'

Bernard slipped the sheaves of banknotes into his briefcase, zipped it, and walked out. The street door clanged behind him – positively for the last time. He made a mental note: Hammet was beginning to see the pattern of his operation, so his name would be struck off the list of prospective buyers. There were plenty of others.

And now to rid himself of the burden of the cash. He looked up at the sky, which had all the moist promise of a brimming bathtub. He could get wet between here and the Post Office, but he'd be lucky to find another vacant parking meter for the Aston. Better to leave it where it was, and walk.

He had brought materials for the job: thick wrapping paper, corrugated card, adhesive tape, string, sealing-wax. Five minutes later he found a quiet spot in the corner of the Post Office, where he made up a neat, brick-shaped parcel of the three hundred and seventy-five twenties. By its looks and weight, it could have been anything from, say, a wad of receipt books to a sample consignment of haberdashery. Or seven thousand, five hundred pounds.

The girl counter clerk accepted it without demur for registered mail. It would be safely in his father's hands by midday tomorrow, Saturday.

The massed clouds had overspilled while he was inside, producing a torrential downpour that was rebounding knee-high and turning the gutters into surging brown rivulets. Bernard remained in the shelter of the Post Office porch, in the company of a pretty young woman in a red plastic mackintosh. She reminded him of the brief life and sudden demise of the new Bernard Davis. He could almost feel the recollection of that little moment of glory generating a spark of unaccustomed valour. The only question being: was it real, or counterfeit; veritable or hallucinatory? Best try it for size. *Toujours de l'audace!*

He cleared his throat. 'Just look at that rain!' he declared.

She gave a small start, and flashed him an interested glance. In an almost indivisible instant of time, the interest dissolved from her expression, and she looked back at the rain-swept street.

He relaxed, defeated. It had ever been thus. They can always tell. Women are born with a built-in mechanism for detecting the mouse within the exterior of the man. Hunching his shoulders, he dug his hands into his coat pockets and, stepping out into the downpour, took flight from the scene of his disastrous small encounter.

The rain had soaked through his coat, and wet him from soles to knees, by the time he reached the Aston, hastily unlocked the door and hurled himself inside. Almost immediately, he smelt tobacco. More precisely – cigar-smell. And he didn't smoke.

Next, he saw the humped shape reflected in the rear-view mirror. The small hairs at the back of his neck were already prickling with sudden shock, as he turned to look at his car rug – a large woolly rectangle of Black Watch tartan that he usually kept in a characteristically neat fold under the rear window – that was now roughly draped over what, from its shape, could only be the figure of a sleeping man.

How the hell had the fellow got in here? Shock turning to indignation, he cried out:

'Hey, you! What in the blazes?...'

He pulled back the edge of the rug, disclosing a tweed-coated back. A plump, round back. Beyond that, a mat

D

of black, wavy hair rolling over the collar.

'Wake up, damn you!'

He pulled at the shoulder, and the form rolled slightly, so that the head came into view.

'Oh, my God! – *Garbisian*!'

The big Armenian was dead; plainly and hideously dead. The eyes were bulging and reddened, staring wildly upwards. The dentures were missing, and the cyanosed tongue lolled out between bare gums of the same hue. Purpled, also, were the heavy cheeks and the rolls of jowl that lapped the shirt collar. It was the face of a hanged man. Garbisian had died choking in agony.

With a shudder, Bernard covered up the terrible head again.

How had it happened? He looked at his own white-faced reflection in the mirror and saw that his lips were trembling. How had the ghastly corpse found its way into the locked car? Who had dumped it here and carelessly thrown the rug on top? He stared ahead, through the streaming windscreen, into the rainswept, empty street, and found no answer. Then he tried the rear door.

The rear door of the Mark III Aston Martin is worked by a lever situated behind the driver's seat, which frees the lock and permits the door to be raised from outside.

Bernard checked the door by pulling the lever. Nothing happened.

He got out into the rain again. Round to the back of the car. And there he saw the answer.

The glass-panelled rear door on the sloping tail of the Aston had been forced. Brutally forced; some specialized thieves' tool had been used to prise it open, and it had then been jammed shut again.

He gave a start of alarm to hear running footsteps, and

turned to see two young girls – city typists, running arm-in-arm, with a single mackintosh over their two heads. As they went past, neither spared a glance for the white-faced man who stood by the peacock-blue car in the streaming gutter.

Bernard ran his hand once more over the edge of the rear door, then went back into the car. He had to think.

Half an hour later the rain had abated and he had run out of time on the parking meter. An attendant was moving slowly down the line of vehicles, notebook in hand, checking. Bernard switched on the powerful engine and snicked off the handbrake.

It had taken him the whole half-hour to come to terms with what might be the truth of the matter, having hedged away from it in horror all the time – in the same way that a person will lie to himself rather than admit fault and destroy his own self-esteem.

He had tried the idea of Garbisian himself forcing open the rear door, then crawling inside to die. The inconsistencies sank that one out of sight. Can a man perform an expert break-in job in his death agony? What compulsion would drive him to it? And why *his* car, of all cars?

He had attempted to fit the Armenian into the role of a suicide, though the recollection of that extrovert, life-loving hedonist of yesterday scarcely made the thought worthy of a moment's consideration. Having forced his way in, how then had Garbisian performed the act? He surely couldn't have throttled himself with his own necktie!

He had toyed with the scene where Garbisian came upon a thief or thieves breaking into the Aston; where a struggle followed, and his friend of yesterday was manually strangled in the affray. But, again, why did it have to be *his* car? Forget that one, also.

Skirt it as he might, evade it for as long as he dare, one factor kept recurring: the connection between him, Bernard Davis (and his car) and Aram Garbisian, former importer and exporter cum theatrical agent. They had met the day before; this morning, Garbisian's dead body was hidden in his car.

And the reason for it? The only one possible: the very reason for his being in London at all: the diamond!

Father's declaration came back to him again: that the Bolsheviks would do anything – *anything* – to get what was left of the treasure he had brought back from Kiev.

Was it not most likely – the most disturbing, but certainly the most probable of all the alternative solutions – that the said Bolsheviks were on to what Father and he were up to, and that Aram Garbisian had, in some way, got himself caught in the crossfire?

The Aston Martin turned into Fleet Street and headed westwards towards the Strand. Having accepted the worst, Bernard now knew his best course of action in what was an extremely narrow field of options: get back to Scunthorpe immediately and get instructions from his father. Before he did anything else – and certainly before he did anything so precipitate as to report Garbisian's death to the police; there was no telling what *that* could lead to. If everything they said about the Bolsheviks was true, it was entirely likely that the dead body lying behind him was planted there to incriminate Bernard Davis on a murder charge! The thought hit him with such force that his foot slipped off the clutch pedal at a pedestrian crossing, and he nearly ploughed into a stout woman pushing a perambulator.

Back to Scunthorpe, that was it. Father would know what to do. He'd know if it was safe to turn Garbisian's body over to the police – or whether it would be best quietly to dispose of the corpse.

The treasure was the key. To safeguard the treasure, Father might decide upon committing what was technically a crime. He was glad that he, Bernard, did not have to make the decision. It was bad enough to be driving towards Charing Cross with a concealed body in the back of his car, instead of shouting the hideous news to the skies.

Blessedly, there was a parking space round the side of his hotel. He got out and locked the car door, checking that the rug-covered shape in the back would not cause a casual passer-by to look twice. On the way through the foyer, approaching the reception desk, he experienced a strange foreboding of disaster – a feeling that he could not entirely attribute to what had already happened.

A counter clerk looked at him enquiringly. 'Sir?'

'My bill, please. I'm leaving right away. Room thirty-six. The name's Davis. B. Davis.'

'Right you are, Mr Davis.' The clerk turned away, and took a sheaf of bills from a pigeon-hole marked 36. And a buff-coloured envelope.

'There's a telegram here for you, sir,' he said.

Bernard knew, then, the nature and quality of the fresh disaster. He knew it with the hard edge of certainty before he ever opened the telegram and stared down at the printed words.

DEEPLY REGRET INFORM YOU FATHER PASSED AWAY PEACEFULLY IN SLEEP EARLY HOURS OF THIS MORN-

ING STOP SUGGEST YOUR IMMEDIATE RETURN — ALEC

The M1 motorway was unwinding underneath him again, and the one whom he had known briefly in life as Aram Garbisian lay in his eternal sleep under the rug, with all the spare clothing from the valise spread all over his stiffening corpse for better concealment.

Mounting a gradient, a slight fluttering in the engine note made Bernard glance down at the instrument panel, where his eye was immediately taken by the fuel warning light. At any other time, he would have spotted it the instant it came on. He switched to the reserve tank. Would that give him enough juice to get home? He thought not — not unless he brought his cruising speed down. Weighing the pros and cons, he decided to put in at the next service station and fill up. The alternative: to run out of petrol on the motorway and have to summon help — with all the concomitant prying eyes — was too risky. His decision was hardened, a few minutes later, by a sign announcing, SERVICES 2M.

Nearly an hour had gone by since Bernard had opened the telegram, and he still had not completely accepted the staggering fact of his father's death. He had telephoned home from the hotel, but the number had remained obstinately engaged. He supposed that he should have tried Alec's or James's home — but it had not occurred to him at the time.

Even a stroke and the resulting two months' confinement in bed had not quenched the truly appalling vitality of the former Prince Davydov, nor modified by a scintilla the total terror and subservience in which the members of his family stood of him. Alone, possibly, of the three brothers, Bernard — because of his special relationship with the old man – had been conscious of an almost imperceptible shift in accent: looking back over those two months, he was able to recall how Father had seemed if anything more imperious and demanding, more the total autocrat; almost as if the savage old lion had felt the need to reassert his mastery over the docile pride.

And now he was gone. The long journey that had begun seventy-six years before in some chandelier-hung bedchamber in the Davydov palace outside Kiev had come to its end. Along the way, the traveller must have known some of the best and the worst that Fate can offer: wealth and privilege in the Court life of Moscow and St Petersburg; the comradeship and hell of a ruinous war; revolution and the loss of his family; exile and memories.

He would miss his father, he – his father's errand boy. But one thing Bernard knew: it was beyond all possibility that he could ever shed a tear, or suffer a pang of grief, for the old devil who had made him into a puppet.

But he would miss him. Already the sense of loss – the feeling of being deprived of that colossal presence – left him panic-stricken.

He was jolted back to reality by the exit road to the services complex immediately ahead. He cut into the slow lane and cleared the motorway. A line of petrol pumps stood beyond a restaurant building. He slowed down and pulled in there.

'Fill her up, please. Where's the telephone?'

The attendant pointed.

He put a call through to Vicarage Gardens, and heard the number ring out. At that moment, from the corner of his eye, he saw a police car glide past the call box and pull up near to the petrol pumps. A tall, blue-clad figure got out from the driver's door, stretched himself, took off his peaked cap and scratched his head.

The ringing tone ceased, and Bernard heard his elder brother's voice announcing the number.

'Alec! It's me – Bernard!'

'I've been trying to reach you all morning. Where are you now?'

'On the motorway. I'll be home in about an hour and a half. Alec, is it really true – he's gone?'

'He's gone, all right. Minna Hodge found him and telephoned me at the office. I immediately...'

Bernard felt his skin crawl. The policeman was looking interestedly towards the Aston. Next, the man straightened his cap and started to walk towards it.

'Can you hear me, Bernard?' Alec's voice took on a petulant tone.

'I can't wait now. Goodbye, Alec!'

'I say!...'

Bernard jammed down the receiver, flung open the call-box door and crossed towards the petrol pumps at a stumbling run. Oh, pray God the policeman doesn't look in the back. If some of Garbisian has become uncovered... it would only need a hand, a foot...

The constable inspected the Aston's radiator, then a front tyre. His expression was grave, critical, professionally guarded. He looked up as Bernard approached. Bernard licked his dry lips and assembled what must surely have been a rictus grin.

'Er, can I help you, Officer?' he asked.

'This your vehicle, sir?'

'Yes.'

The constable ran his hand across the long bonnet, fondly.

'Lovely motor,' he said. 'It was always my favourite, the Mark Three. Fetching very high prices now, so I hear. My brother-in-law let one go for seven hundred quid ten years ago. Reckons it'd cost him twice that to buy it back again now. Crazy world, isn't it?'

'Crazy,' echoed Bernard. The pump attendant had finished, and he handed him a couple of five-pound notes. The man ambled slowly over to the cash desk to get his change.

'This brother-in-law of mine,' said the policeman, 'used to go out in the Aston with my sister, with the baby in a carrycot in the back, plus a folding pram, and bring home a week's shopping as comfortable as you please. Why, there's not many family saloons can cope with that, let alone sports cars. I see you've got a good load on today, sir.'

'I – I've been to London for a couple of days,' said Bernard, with a desperate glance towards the cash desk, where the attendant was deep in grinning conversation with a girl at the till.

The constable was now stooping low to peer in the side windows towards the back; towards the humped shape under the tartan rug that shrieked its guilty secret with every nuance of line and form. And the dirty linen strewn over the top: paradoxically, this worried Bernard as much as anything, striking as it did at his compulsive tidiness.

'Terrible mess, I'm afraid,' he said apologetically. 'I left my hotel in rather a hurry and just threw my things in the back.'

'Oh yes,' nodded his companion. Then he walked round the rear end of the car – and saw where the door had been wrenched open. 'Hello! You had a bit of trouble, sir?'

'It's nothing,' Bernard hastened to tell him.

'I wouldn't call it nothing, sir. Messing up a lovely car like this. When did it happen?'

'Oh, this morning . . .'

The constable's eyes came up to meet his. The expression was quite different from what it had been.

'This is a professional break-in job, sir,' he said quietly. 'You can see the marks of the jemmy. You reported it, of course?'

'No – I – I didn't have time this morning.' A sidelong glance told him that the attendant had got his change and was slowly walking back.

The policeman took a notebook and pencil from his breast pocket, still eyeing Bernard with professional blankness.

'If I could just have a look at your driving licence and insurance cover note, sir,' he said. 'Then, if you'll give me the details of the break-in, please . . .'

It had to be gone through, right to the bitter end. By the finish of it, Bernard was almost past caring; he was within an ace of confessing – if only to assure himself that the whole thing was not some ghastly charade concocted by a faceless, omnipotent and sadistic Authority; and that the policeman, who was using the smooth top of the Aston as a surface on which to rest his notebook, was not thoroughly aware that the dead, strangled face of the Armenian was only inches beneath his hands.

When he had taken Bernard's statement, the other

said: 'Right, sir, this'll be passed on to London. Don't suppose anything will come of it, particularly since you say nothing was nicked, but it might be a piece of evidence that will fit into a larger pattern, if you follow my meaning.'

'I think I understand, Officer,' said Bernard meekly. 'Can I go now?'

'Please proceed, sir,' replied the other, saluting. And, as Bernard revved up the engine and let in the clutch, he leaned in through the driver's window and gave a 'thumb's up' sign. 'Lovely motor-car, sir. Smashing. Quite made my day.'

And mine, thought Bernard ruefully. This Friday the Thirteenth is going to be one to remember!

He was aware, from a careful glance in his rear-view mirror, that a small yellow Fiat saloon followed him out of the services area and on to the motorway; but thought nothing of it till it became obvious that the Fiat's driver was using the blue Aston Martin as a pacemaker; slotting in behind the sports car about fifty yards to the rear and overtaking slower vehicles in the same pattern – a common enough practice in long-distance motorway driving, particularly among those psychologically better-adjusted members of the road-using fraternity who do not have the compulsion to overtake everything in sight. On a normal occasion, Bernard would have registered the fact and then have dismissed it.

This was no normal occasion.

He was, perhaps, being followed. The Bolsheviks were trailing him; and if not the Bolsheviks, who else? Checking, no doubt, to see what means he would use to dispose of the body with which they had lumbered him! As far as Bernard could make out (for the Fiat never came closer than fifty yards, and slackened and quickened pace with him), there was only the driver in the other car. He determined to put his theory to the test, and also to get close enough for a look at his pursuer's face — but without raising any undue suspicion in the other's mind that his presence was either detected or was causing any great concern to the pursued.

When the next services complex came up, Bernard made an early and very deliberate signal and turned on to the exit road. Amber winker flashing, the Fiat came after him. Bernard brought the Aston to the parking area in front of the cafeteria building, and there he waited till the yellow saloon had found a space some distance to the rear. He then got out of the car and walked towards the cafeteria entrance. Half-way there, as if suddenly struck with a recollection, he stopped and looked at his watch; went through a brief pantomime of indecision, and turned back to the Aston. From the corner of his eye, he saw that the driver of the Fiat had stayed in the car.

Quickly gunning the engine, Bernard sent it back in reverse, till he was level with the Fiat. Then, just as he was about to go forward again in the direction of the exit road, he gave a casual glance towards the other driver.

What he saw was a pair of all-concealing dark glasses set on a woman's face. The hair was out of sight: piled under a beret. The face told him nothing, and slowly turned to look away. No embarrassment there.

The Fiat followed him out on to the motorway again, but did not remain in sight for long. Taking the chance of being picked up by a police patrol, Bernard drove his foot down hard on the accelerator, and the Aston Martin responded nobly. Not till the yellow dot had faded away far to the rear did he slow down to the regulation seventy miles an hour.

It was one-thirty by his dashboard clock when, Doncaster past behind, he saw the smoking chimneys and three high-rise apartment buildings of Scunthorpe coming up out of the flat landscape ahead.

Alec Davis's funereal saloon stood outside his father's house in Vicarage Gardens, where all the curtains were drawn as a mark of mourning. Minna Hodge opened the door to Bernard before he reached the step. The woman had been crying. He nodded a greeting to her; there was so little of human contact between them that it scarcely seemed relevant to exchange the conventional expressions of grief and regret that the situation called for.

'Mr Alec and his wife are upstairs,' said the woman flatly. 'With the master,' she added. 'Have you had anything to eat? There's a pork pie, or I could do you a bit of a fry-up.'

'No, thanks. I've eaten,' lied Bernard, climbing the stairs.

The door of his father's bedroom was ajar, and through it came the faint, sickly scent of arum lilies, which he detested. The curtained gloom was lightened only by the flickering glow of tall candles that stood sentinel, one each side of the bed, upon which lay the late, former Prince Vladimir Ilich Davydov.

Two black-garbed figures standing at the foot of the bed turned when he entered: Alec and his wife.

Alec glanced crossly at his younger brother. Kitty's

plain, doughy countenance was seraphic with spiritual enthusiasm.

'We've prepared the room as a *chapelle ardente*,' she whispered. 'The Prince will lie here in state till the day of interment.'

Bernard glanced about him in the scented murk. The tall brass candlesticks must have come from the firm's Chapel of Rest in Doncaster Road, likewise the tall vases for the lilies. The icons at the bedhead were part of the vast collection that cluttered Alec and Kitty's house. Heaven only knew where they had found the framed photograph of Nicholas II that hung immediately behind the corpse's head.

His father looked curiously small and – for the first time ever – not at all frightening.

'Lovely, isn't it?' whispered Kitty. 'A true memory of Holy Russia that I'm sure the Prince would have appreciated.'

Bernard glanced at his brother and made no comment. Alec looked away, embarrassed – as well he might be, knowing as he did that, whatever their father's private memories, he had never expressed any particular affection for Holy Russia, the last of the Romanoffs, or indeed for anything connected with the land of his birth save tea made in a samovar and an occasional glass of vodka.

'I must go now,' said Kitty. 'I have to get Maria and Anastasia their lunch.'

'Take the car,' said Alec. 'I'll walk home when I've talked to Bernard.'

'All right,' said his wife. 'I'll leave you two together to pay your filial respects.' She pecked her husband on the cheek. 'See you later . . . Prince,' she murmured tremulously.

Oh, my God, thought Bernard. It's started. The old man not yet cold, but we're all princes and princesses already.

Kitty's footfalls faded away in silence down the stairs, and they heard the front door close.

They both turned to regard the still form on the bed.

Presently, Alec said: 'Well, he's gone. I don't know what we shall do now. Carry on as usual, I suppose. Too late for changes now.'

'Changes?' Bernard glanced sharply at his brother.

'I wanted to be a doctor,' said Alec. 'You never knew that, did you? But he stopped all that. That would have made me too independent of him. The same with James. James wanted to go to college and be a schoolteacher, but it had to be the bloody family undertaking business for the two of us.' He shot Bernard a resentful glare. 'No Oxford and a literary career for *us*!'

'I'm sorry, Alec,' said Bernard. 'I really am. But it's not the way you think. Father may have seemed to have let me go my own way, but I've never really stepped outside the reach of his hand. I've been more of a prisoner than you have.'

They stood in silence for a while, each with his own thoughts, looking down at the waxen face of their dead sire.

'I've arranged for the funeral for Tuesday,' said Alec. 'The firm will conduct it, of course. It'll be a Church of England service, since Father's never shown any religious tendencies and I can't lay my hands on a Russian Orthodox priest. Oh, and I've been in touch with the solicitor. Father left a will.'

'You think of everything,' said Bernard with no sense of sarcasm.

'Someone has to,' said Alec. 'The will is going to be read on Tuesday, after the interment. It'll be a pure formality, of course. I've already ascertained that, as you might expect, Father left his entire estate to be divided between the three of us. I estimate that, with the business and various properties, it amounts to around a hundred and fifty thousand – on which there'll be death duties to pay, of course.'

Bernard dragged his gaze away from the dead, white face on the bed. The panic-stricken feeling of deprivation had been exorcised by the presence of the autocrat's lifeless image. He was still alone, and the thought filled him with dread – but also with a wayward feeling of elation.

'He left more than that, Alec,' he said to his brother. 'More than you know – and a hell of a lot of trouble. Trouble that I can't begin to see the end of!'

'What the blazes do you mean?' demanded the other.

Then Bernard told him – everything.

'But what are we going to *do*?'

They had retired downstairs to the drawing-room, where Alec was steadying his nerves with a second large scotch. The long history of the treasure had come as a traumatic shock to the elder brother; when he had heard about the corpse in the back of the Aston Martin, Bernard had thought he was going to collapse.

'Keep it between the two of us, for a start,' said Bernard. 'Father was right in confiding only in me – the fewer people who know the secret, the better. So we don't even tell James. By the way, where is James?'

'He's working,' said Alec. 'We're snowed under with jobs this week. All right, we keep it to ourselves. Then what?'

'Get rid of that body,' said Bernard. 'I thought it over carefully on the way home. Whoever Garbisian was and whatever reason the Bolsheviks had for killing him, the body was dumped in my car to embarrass me – that's to say us, the former Davydovs, the holders of the secret hoard of treasure that Father brought out of Russia in 'nineteen. So our logical response should be to rid ourselves of the gratuitous embarrassment.'

'But we don't *have* the treasure!' cried Alec.

'It's around somewhere,' said Bernard. 'We shall come across it, sooner or later. Knowing Father, you can be sure he made some provision for me to find it after his death.'

'All right. What do we do with a dead body in a place like Scunthorpe?' demanded Alec.

'Bury it,' said his brother calmly. 'That's why I've brought you into the secret. You're an undertaker.'

'Bury it *where*?'

'In a graveyard, along with all the rest.'

'You're insane!' cried Alec. 'If Father had made you come into the business instead of letting you waste your time in scribbling, you'd know that you can't go around burying *any* old body. There are such things as death certificates. Next of kin. Mourners. Man, you've no idea what a serious business it is to die in this country.'

'We'll get round it somehow,' said Bernard. Heavens, he thought to himself, I really am taking this situation calmly. Who would have thought it of nervous old Bernard? Rising to the crisis like this. And he went on: 'Maybe we'll have to forge a death certificate. We can be his mourners and next of kin. We could even put him in a coffin with a genuine death-certificated corpse and bury them together.'

'Two in one coffin?' wailed Alec. 'Now I *know* you're insane! This business has turned your brain!'

'It would have to be a pretty light corpse, the other one,' mused Bernard, unperturbed by his brother's outburst. 'Garbisian must weight all of sixteen stone. We'll have to think of something else. There's plenty of time. The main thing is to get the body out of the back of my car and safely under lock and key in your mortuary. I suppose you've got refrigeration?'

'Fitch, Davis and Sons have all the latest modern undertaking amenities,' said Alec with some asperity and almost a touch of pride. 'Including individual drawer-style refrigeration compartments that will keep the cadaver for an almost indefinite period.'

'Are these drawers kept locked?' asked Bernard.

'Always,' responded his brother. 'The custodianship of the departed is a sacred trust,' he added primly.

'Good,' said Bernard. 'It'll be well dark by seven. I'll bring the Aston round to the back entrance of the mortuary at seven. Have the gates open for me then. We'll put poor Garbisian away in your filing cabinet till we can think of a permanent way to dispose of him. And now I need a drink.'

In the event, the remains of Aram Garbisian were fated not to be moved from their resting-place that fateful Friday the Thirteenth.

Bernard spent the afternoon making as thorough a search as he could of his father's house, but in this enterprise was inhibited by the presence of Minna Hodge. He informed the housekeeper that he was looking for some of the old man's papers, an explanation that she received with the deepest suspicion. At a quarter to seven, he quit trying to find a clue to the whereabouts of the treasure and drove the Aston to a cul-de-sac at the rear of the family undertaker's establishment in Doncaster Road, where Alec was already waiting by the open gates that led into the yard.

The gates safely closed and bolted, the brothers prepared to take out the body of the Armenian. This meant opening the rear door of the Aston; a problem that Bernard attempted to overcome from the inside by reaching over the humped corpse and trying to release the catch.

'I can't do it,' he said at length. 'The swine jammed it down so hard when they forced it shut that it's completely seized up. We'll have to bring him out the front, it's basically no more difficult.'

In this glib assumption, Bernard was entirely mistaken, as he discovered as soon as he removed the coverings from the corpse and tried to turn it. He cried out in horror.

'What's happened?' asked Alec.

'He's as stiff as a board!' cried Bernard, 'and bent up all ways, like a blessed swastika. We'd scarcely have been able to get him out the back. The front way's completely out of the question.'

'Let me have a look,' said Alec, elbowing his brother aside. 'You're right. He's stuck there till the rigor mortis wears off.'

'When will that be?' cried Bernard.

'Depends on several factors, principally the temperature of the external environment,' said Alec the undertaker. 'But it won't be before tomorrow. Not in this weather.'

'Tomorrow!' cried Bernard. 'Don't tell me I've got

to keep him hidden in my car till it's dark again tomorrow evening?'

'You might just as well,' said his brother unfeelingly. 'Even if we could get him out of here, we wouldn't be able to put him into the refrigeration cabinet till the rigor's gone. Not in that state.' Professional dignity rising above the terrors of the situation, he added: 'Why, he's not been properly laid out.'

'I've no doubt his murderer or murderers would have laid him out according to the book and put pennies on his eyes,' snarled Bernard. 'But it was raining at the time, and they were in a hurry!'

So Aram Garbisian spent his first night of organic death in the street behind Bernard's flat, close by the windows of the Cathay Flower restaurant, all unseen and unsuspected by the diligent Chinese, as they laboured over their crab foo yung and their crispy pancake rolls.

CHAPTER V

The view from the long window of the sixth-floor conference-room looked out across the wide street to one of Washington's most renowned hotels, in whose forecourt had been placed a Christmas tree of winking lights and glittering baubles. A despondent Santa Claus kept vigil by the tree, stamping his feet and blowing on his hands to combat the biting cold. Above his head, a loud-speaker played, through and through, an endless recording of 'Silent Night'. When the conference started, someone suggested drawing the heavy window drapes, to cut down some of the joyous sound. It worked pretty well.

Chairing the meeting was a fairly high-grade person named Steiner. Present also was Williams of the Department, his aides, and people from various other agencies, most of whom were known to one another. Twelve in all, including the stenographer.

The former Tsarist Russia (Residuals) Section was not represented at the meeting, since the subject under discussion was one which was deemed to have risen out of their orbit. It was whispered around the agencies that what had come to be known as the Davydov Situation had become a very big band-wagon indeed – and that Williams was riding shotgun.

The chairman opened the proceedings with the right touch of informality by inviting anyone to smoke who wished, then he introduced Williams and asked him to start the ball rolling.

'Ah, Mr Chairman, I'd like to open the discussion at this time by recapitulating the situation as I appreciated it in June last,' said Williams.

'I think that is absolutely on all fours, Mr Williams,' indicated the chairman. 'Please proceed along those lines.'

'The situation as I appreciated it in June last,' said Williams, 'and I may say at this time that I was greatly assisted in my deliberations by the splendid, I should say outstanding, field-work of Dade and his aide DeSoto in uncovering the facts of this growing situation – the situation as I appreciated it in June last is one for whose veracity I take total responsibility.' He was a heavily-built, square-jawed man, and no one met his eye as he glared challengingly round the table. 'I'd like to bring you all to a focus on this: the initiative for action on the

Davydov situation was mine and mine alone. If it all gets loused up, if I'm off base, it'll be my head on the block.'

'Mr Chairman, if I may interject?' This was Jackson, who was one of Williams's principal aides. 'Since Joe here is laying his reputation on the line, I'd like to go on record as saying that he had my full support in this situation from the first, and still has. If we're wrong in this, I want to share the blame.'

'I appreciate that, Tom,' said Williams coldly.

'We're all in this together, Joe.'

'Nice of you to say so, Tom.'

'If that's established, gentlemen,' said the chairman, 'may we proceed?'

'Mr Chairman,' continued Williams. 'As to the background, I think it is going to be of aid if I ask Don Arkle of my staff to read out part of my appreciation of the situation, my scenario of June last, that deals with my first premise in some regards.'

The chairman nodded assent, and a young aide took a thick, calf-bound folder from his briefcase and put on a pair of glasses.

'We'll get past this in a hurry, Mr Chairman,' said Williams. 'Just so we cover the situation all the way down the line. Go right ahead, Don.'

'Yes, sir,' said Don Arkle, and he began reading:
' "Properly to appreciate the Davydov Situation, one has got to look back over the total record of British diplomacy and the traditional means by which the former British Empire gained its ends. These included not only straightforward diplomacy, but also assassination, judicial murder, suborning by bribery, kidnapping, character-assassination, and conventional war. Also – and this is relevant in the context of the present situation – by the

method of setting up puppet rulers and governments in states outside the jurisdiction of the British Empire, in order to facilitate the absorbing of these states into the jurisdiction of the British Empire. It was the method of the Fifth Column, and it would be true to say that it was not General Mola before Madrid who devised the expedient of the Fifth Column, but British diplomatists of the nineteenth century and earlier.

' "The Fifth Column principle, of setting up puppet rulers and governments by the British, can be traced right back to their former Empire's beginnings. Here, in alphabetical order, follows a brief summary . . .

' "In the case of Afghanistan: the British imposed Shah Shuja on the unwilling people of that country, and he was crowned in Kabul during the Afghan War of eighteen . . ." '

'Mr Williams,' interposed the chairman. ' I won't critique your historical researches into the past perfidies of the British, for I know they must be impeccable; and I don't want to gloss the background to the situation, nor your part in bringing it to the fore; but can we not rapidly advance to your first premise in this thing, and thence to the turn the situation has taken at this present time – which is the reason for this conference being convened?'

'Damn right, Mr Chairman,' said Williams stoutly. 'Briefly, sir, my appreciation of June last – which has now been borne out by events – was that the British Government was secretly moving to set up the House of Davydov as heirs and successors to the House of Romanoff, in respect of that part of present Soviet territory designated the Ukraine. In short, to set the Davydovs up as *de jure* rulers of the Ukraine.'

'But not in order to facilitate the absorbing of the Ukraine into British jurisdiction?' asked the chairman with a smile.

'Indeed no, sir,' frowned Williams.

'You'll pardon my little joke, Joe.'

'You knocked the hell out from under me there, Sam,' grinned Williams, and a chuckle was passed around the table. 'No, the motivation is different, though what I would call the atavistic response is the same as in earlier situations. My scenario is that the British are putting up the Davydovs to burn the tail of the Soviets in time for next year's Worldwide Energy Convention. They hope to use the Soviets' embarrassment as a bargaining factor. If the Limeys can get their hooks on some of that Volga-Urals oil in the course of the convention, they'll no doubt agree to deport the House of Davydov to Moscow – and to liquidation.'

A murmur of righteous indignation rippled round the table, for though some were hearing the scenario for the tenth time, others were hearing it for the first.

'You think the British will go so far out on a limb, behind the backs of the rest of the Free World, to make an independent oil deal with the Soviets?'

'Damn right I do, Mr Chairman!' replied Williams. 'I covered that whole contingency, up one side and down the other, in my appreciation of June last. And the outstanding field-work of Dade and DeSoto – to which I've already paid high tribute – ties this thing down in many regards.'

'Specifically?'

'Specifically in the area of the Davydov family reaction to the situation, Mr Chairman. The wife of the eldest son and ruler-designate is openly boasting of the forthcoming elevation. Mrs Kitty Davis – who has called herself Princess Ekaterina Davydov since her father-in-law's decedency at – ah – approximately three o'clock, Greenwich Mean Time, in the morning of Friday the thirteenth – went so far as secretly to order the manufacture of two silver-gilt coronets, set with cultured pearls and semiprecious stones, for herself and her husband. We have a true copy of the receipt. *And this was in May last!*'

'Mr Chairman, if I may interject?' It was the faithful Jackson again. 'Ah, you won't want to get tied down with details at this present time, but in support of Joe's scenario, Dade and DeSoto came across with around fifty specific items with regard to Davydov family reactions, etcetera, etcetera. And these are mere titbits compared with what has been uncovered in this developing situation.'

The chairman brightened up. 'Like I pointed out in the beginning, gentlemen,' he said, with a glance at his wristwatch, 'it was on account of the developing situation that this conference was convened. Now, I have listened with some patience to a recapitulation of the beginning situation . . .'

'I may be off base, Mr Chairman,' interrupted Williams vehemently, 'but I thought I had made it abundantly clear in the outset that my motive for recapitulation was to point out that the initiative for action in the Davydov Situation was mine – ' he glanced fiercely round the assembled gathering, pausing for a lingering moment at his faithful aide Jackson – '*all* mine!'

'That's quite clear, Joe,' purred the chairman placatingly.

'And we're all right behind you, Joe,' said the imperturbable Jackson.

'I call upon Mr Arthur Seymour,' said the chairman hastily, 'of the Surveillance Section, to report on the developing situation. Go right ahead, Arthur.'

Mr Arthur Seymour was a young, brisk ex-Rhodes scholar, who wore a Savile Row suit and a necktie emblazoned with the arms of Oxford University. He read his report in a marked British accent and at a smart trot.

' "Acting upon the Department's decision," ' he read, ' "an immediate, close surveillance was put upon the Davydov-Davis family. The situation was thoroughly checked out. It was worse than we thought. Not only did the situation exist, as suggested in the scenario, but we were far from first in the field. In fact, I would go so far as to say that we are possibly around the last of the major powers to appraise ourselves of the Davydov Situation!" '

This last remark brought an instant reaction of horror and amazement from all present.

'Who else has gotten in on the act?' demanded the chairman.

'Certainly the Soviets, Mr Chairman,' said Seymour. 'The British, of course. Maybe the French and the West Germans. One of our field agents, now I put it really hard to him by telephone on the twelfth, and he implied very strongly that the French and the West Germans have also gotten very close to the developing Davydov Situation.'

'And now we hear,' said the chairman, 'that someone pulled the plug on this guy, this Garbisian?'

'That is so, sir. Garbisian went missing while keeping a tail on Bernard Davis, and it is our opinion that he is not alive at this time.'

'You mean,' asked Williams, 'you mean that he was rubbed out and the body disposed of; or that he was kidnapped and questioned, maybe tortured, etcetera, etcetera?'

'Either of those two options, sir,' replied Seymour.

'And, if tortured, do you think he caved?'

'Undoubtedly, sir,' said Seymour coolly. 'Garbisian would sing like a bird, but he was only possessed of very low classification information. And knew no details of the Davydov Situation *per se*.'

'Who did it, Arthur?' This from the chairman.

Seymour shrugged his shoulders. 'The British, on account of him getting too close. The Soviets, for getting in their way. No telling, sir.'

'What type guy was this Garbisian? Was he an American citizen?'

Seymour looked embarrassed. 'Ah – his status was that of a stateless person, sir. He entered Britain two years ago under a forged passport from Malta, and has worked for us ever since, under – ah – certain inducements. He was not a very edifying type guy, and he had been thrown out of Egypt for pimping.'

'What were these inducements, Arthur?'

Seymour coloured. 'We – ah – gave him to understand that, the situation permitting it, he might one day be allowed immigrancy facilities to this country. That was his greatest ambition.'

'Did we have any intention, Arthur, of implementing this proposal?' asked the chairman quietly.

'Not at any future time, sir,' replied the young man from the Surveillance Section.

There was a silence; and then:

'Gentlemen,' said the chairman, 'I would like to throw the rest of this meeting open to a brain session, which I think will be of great aid in getting this situation back on its feet again. May I now hear your proposals?'

'Mr Chairman,' said Jackson, with one eye on his chief, Williams. 'We want to pay just as little price as we can in this situation, and let's hope that minimal people will be hurt. I'm proposing that, as a precaution, we should advise the Secretary of State to have the Sixth Fleet move to Gibraltar.'

'You really think the development could move along those lines, Tom?' asked the chairman with respect and some awe.

'I think Joe Williams's foresight in predicting the Davydov Situation has maybe saved next year's World-wide Energy Convention,' replied the other. 'Now I think we should put some teeth in support of Joe's great initiative.'

Pink with pure pleasure, Williams threw his aide a look of deep affection.

There were three in the office, which had been the main salon of a former Imperial residence in the Rokossovsky Prospect: a bearded individual of about forty, named Glinka; a uniformed major in his early thirties, called Kornilov; and the Controller, whose office it was.

Glinka and Kornilov had just been summoned. They stood before the desk, looking down upon the Controller's bent head with its coarse black hair shot with white, and at the powerful fingers gripping pen and cigarette.

There was an oil painting of Marx over the ornate chimney-piece, a massive composition representing Lenin addressing a crowd of workers and soldiers on the longest wall opposite the tall windows that looked out over the Prospect. Lighter patches on the dirty white panelling showed where artworks of a less edifying nature had long since been removed. The Controller's fur-lined overcoat hung from a government pattern hat-stand. The goloshes that stood underneath dribbled a puddle of melted snow.

The Controller sat back and snapped shut a file. The antiquated central heating system left the room chill. Glinka could see that she was not wearing a brassière under the thick woollen shirt.

'You realize that this is a crisis situation!' the Controller began without any preamble, her square, doughy-white face totally devoid of expression.

Glinka cleared his throat and said nervously: 'I suppose, Comrade Controller, that there is no chance of a misapprehension?'

Her small eyes, like the pebbles of a dull blue glass that you find in the surf, favoured Glinka with only the briefest glance.

'There is no possibility of misapprehension,' she said flatly. 'The Archives Department has recorded every known item of pre-Revolution property above the intrinsic value of ten thousand roubles. The item in question was photographed – in monochrome, of course – during an inventory carried out at the orders of the Metropolitan Archbishop of Kiev in nineteen-sixteen. We possess an excellent print. The six individual gems – four diamonds and two rubies – which have found their way into our possession, through the world markets, in the last thirty years, have clearly been identified from the print as having come from the item in question. We have known for a long time that the item still existed somewhere beyond the borders of the USSR – and now we know in whose possession, if not precisely where . . .' so saying, she took from a cotton wool-lined box an object which she placed on her palm and held under the desk lamp. A million pin-points of fiery light sprang from the diamond's faceted heart. 'This latest gem to have been prised from the missing item was sold by the subject Bernard Davis, in London, on the thirteenth.'

Major Kornilov shifted his stance, and his well-boned boots creaked. 'Surely that is a matter for some congratulation, in any event,' he ventured.

The cold pebble eyes looked up from the gem.

'The operation was botched,' she grated. 'Have the agents been recalled and questioned?'

'I interrogated them myself last night, as soon as their aircraft landed,' said the major hastily.

'And? . . .'

'Briefly, it appears that they followed Bernard Davis to Hatton Garden, where they observed him enter a dealer's establishment and later depart. Immediately after, the subject Garbisian entered the establishment. Our men followed him, and were in time to overhear Garbisian making an offer to the dealer for whatever it was that Bernard Davis had just sold to him. In fact, the dealer had the stone in his hand when our men entered.'

'Were they carrying guns?' demanded the Controller.

'No,' replied Kornilov. 'They state that it was the dealer who, taking fright, produced a pistol and attempted to telephone for the police. There was a brief struggle. Our men overpowered the dealer and disarmed him.'

'And killed Garbisian,' finished the Controller. 'In direct contravention of express orders to keep this affair at a low key, they killed.'

'They deny intention to kill,' said Major Kornilov. 'They claim that Garbisian had some kind of seizure during a manual affray. I shall resume the interrogation after they have both recovered consciousness.'

'In any event,' said the Controller, 'the dealer was neutralized, and the diamond obtained.'

'That part was handled immediately and most discreetly by our special London staff,' said Kornilov. 'For the consideration of fifty thousand pounds sterling, deposited in his name in a Swiss bank account, the dealer Hammet was only too pleased to hand over the diamond and forget the whole occurrence.'

The Controller nodded, and made a note on her pad. 'I think, notwithstanding,' she said, 'it would be prudent if the dealer Hammet were very shortly to be the victim of a fatal road accident. You will attend to this, Comrade Glinka.'

'Yes, Comrade Controller,' said Glinka hastily. He had all this while been listening to the major's report with visible and growing concern.

'As you are aware, Comrade Controller,' said Kornilov, 'the body of Garbisian was immediately disposed of by being put into Bernard Davis's automobile.'

'In many ways the best solution,' said the woman. 'It will provide a considerable problem for the Davis family, coming as it does on the heels of the old man's death. Now, see here, Glinka . . .'

'Yes, Comrade Controller?' said Glinka, his fingers plucking nervously at the straggly ends of his beard.

'You will be held directly responsible for the further outcome of this operation – as, indeed, you are held responsible for what has happened so far. In a sense, Glinka, you are being given the opportunity to put your house in order.'

'Thank you, Comrade Controller.'

'The item in question – at present in the possession of the former Davydov family – must either be recovered, or it must be totally destroyed.'

'Recovered, or totally destroyed. Yes.'

'To this end, Glinka, you will send only the very best of our people, and all fully briefed. Not like the others. And you will inform our agent in Scunthorpe, England, that these people are coming.'

'Immediately, Comrade Controller.'

'I repeat again – the item must be recovered or totally destroyed – as, for illustration, being deposited in a deep part of the North Sea. There is no assessing the chaos that item would cause if, for instance, the capitalist powers of the West smuggled it back into the Ukraine, where it went underground – to become an object of veneration by the superstitious peasantry, causing widespread dislocation and disaffection; perhaps, even, a rallying point for counter-revolutionary forces.'

'You really think,' breathed Glinka, 'you really think, and the Party Presidium really thinks – dear me, it is truly astonishing – that the miraculous powers of that object? . . .'

For the first time during the interview, the woman's eyes flared widely, and an expression approximating to emotion flickered briefly across her pasty countenance.

'What are you trying to say, Glinka?' she whispered.

'Why, Comrade Controller,' faltered that unfortunate, 'I am referring to the supernatural powers with which the thing has always been attributed. There may be something in it, of course. These superstitions often spring from a grain of truth. But I never would have believed that you, Comrade Controller, let alone the Party Presidium, would have embraced . . .' his words tailed off to silence, as he became fully aware of the effect they were having upon the woman behind the desk. Major Kornilov, meanwhile, was staring at him with the sort of horrified distaste, totally unmixed with compassion, with which one regards the mangled victim of a particularly unpleasant road smash.

There was a long silence, broken only by the popping and wheezing of the antiquated central heating system.

Presently, the woman said: 'What is your background, Comrade Glinka?'

'I – I'm from Novgorod, Comrade Controller,' breathed Glinka in a dying voice.

'Family living?'

'Mother and sister. I – I am unmarried, Comrade Controller.' His voice expired with the last syllable.

She made a short note on her pad.

'You may go and make the arrangements for the continuation of the operation, Comrade Glinka,' she said.

Glinka blinked at her, nodded, and walked away unseadily down the long room to the door.

When it had shut behind him, the Controller said: 'I think I must recommend that several fleet units, both surface and submarine, be moved into the proximity with the England east coast, in the River Humber area.'

A strident tap upon the door.

'Come!'

The newcomer entered. He wore a three-piece suit of clerical grey, with a slender watch chain hung across his waistcoat, and a discreet red carnation in his buttonhole. Fair hair worn straight and long in the neck; nice teeth. He was Bimbo to his friends, who were legion.

'Saturday is absolute hell in this place,' he said, 'with

F

everyone gorn to the country. Did I hear you wanted to see me?'

'Yes, Bimbo. Can't seem to recall what it was now.' The speaker was seated in a wing armchair by the fire, smoking a cigar and reading *The Times*. He was a few years older than Bimbo – in his late forties; identically dressed, but without a carnation. He was known to his intimates as Booters.

'How was the party?' asked Bimbo, helping himself to a cigarette from the silver box on the leather-topped desk.

'Average. The Minister got very biddy and sang "The Red Flag". He was with difficulty restrained from putting ice cubes down the Ambassadress's front. He really will have to go.'

'What can one expect? Bus driver to Minister of the Crown in five easy lessons? Booters, if there's nothing doing this afternoon, do you mind awfully if I push orf? There's a point-to-point and m' brother-in-law might romp home in the third race.'

'By all means do, Bimbo. And put a pony on him for me, will you? Now, what was it I wanted to talk to you about?'

'Do you suppose it was business, Booters?'

'I suppose it must have been . . .' Booters drew on his cigar and gazed reflectively into the heart of the fire.

'Anything to do with the latest batch of telegrams?'

'Why yes, it was. How very bright of you.' Booters uncoiled his elegant length from the chair, crossed over to his desk and took up a sheaf of buff-coloured forms from a tray marked *Some Day Maybe*, that stood next a tray similarly labelled (and, let it be known, both in jest), *Seldom, if Ever*.

'Do we have trouble?' asked Bimbo.

'Murmurings from Moscow,' said the other. 'A lot of signal traffic, and they've whipped home two of their people – of the rubber-mackintosh-and-cauliflower-ear-brigade – in rather a hurry. They arrived in Moscow on a scheduled flight, under escort, where they were immediately interrogated by none other than Kornilov.'

'Kornilov,' said Bimbo, 'once made a very heavy pass at m' sister at Henley Regatta. Anything else?'

'Yes. The Yanks have lost one of their people in London. Washington is running round in circles about it to what seems a disproportionate degree. He went missing Friday.'

'Do we know him?'

'Garbisian.'

'*Garbisian*? Not the chap who exports Ladies' Palm Court Orchestras to fates worse than death in Beirut?'

'The very same.'

'The Yanks can't *really* be serious about Garbisian. Why, we've been unloading the most transparent hogwash on Garbisian for years.'

'Odd, isn't it?' said Booters. 'That's why I thought I'd like a word with you. I mean, in your opinion, do you think it's worth passing this stuff on down the line – it being the weekend and all, and so near to Christmas?'

'There are a lot of people,' said Bimbo, 'who aren't going to be frightfully pleased about having their pheasant shootin' interrupted.'

'Quite,' concurred Booters. 'I'll take note of your advice, Bimbo, and perhaps sleep on it. We don't want to get the home team's knickers in a twist over nothing. Have a good weekend. See you on Tuesday.'

''Bye, dear boy,' said Bimbo. 'I won't forget to put your pony on Tony.' He got to the door, and then turned.

'I'm sure you're right, not to be goin' orf at half-cock about that Garbisian business, Booters.'

'Absolutely,' replied his colleague. 'I'm sure it's nothing.'

'Nothing ever happens around here.'

'The bloody place,' said Booters, 'has never been the same since Kim went over the wall.'

CHAPTER VI

Bernard Davis's awakening, on the morning of Saturday the fourteenth, was informed by a curious sense of well-being that was not immediately dissipated by the gradual unfolding of present truths – unfolding, layer by layer, like onion skins, the way memory returns after profound sleep – about his life.

Not even the remembrance of the horror that lay in the back of the Aston Martin could dispel the vague feeling of euphoria with which he gazed out across the rooftops of the town and watched storm clouds massing over the grey estuary to the north-east; nor did the recollection of his father's demise quench the wayward thought that, though suddenly hedged in by matters of heavy gravity, he was nevertheless going to find the means to cope with them.

The new Bernard Davis resurrected? Something like that. He thought back to the episode in his London hotel room, and was able to smile. Given the way he felt this morning, the outcome of his encounter with that girl – what was her name? Janice – would take a very different course, if it could only be translated to here and now.

He stripped to his skin for his shower and gave himself a look-over in the long mirror. Yes, he really was in very good shape for a forty-two-year-old: not an ounce of flab, but not skinny either.

His euphoria took a slight knock when he found that he must have left his electric razor back in the London hotel; as he had no spare, it meant waiting till the shops opened before he had any means of ridding himself of a heavy stubble. Or he could grow a beard. Father had never liked beards: once when he had attempted to grow one, the old man had threatened to cut off his allowance, a threat before which he had had to capitulate – and he over thirty at that time.

Yes, definitely, things were going to be very different now that Father had gone.

He selected a white shirt, and was knotting a black silk tie at his throat, when he heard a car pull up outside, and saw Monica getting out of the passenger seat. She wore a suède leather coat with a fur collar that gave her a particularly soft and feminine appearance. Her cheeks were glowing with the effect of the chill wind that suddenly met her. The phrase came to his mind: 'wild rose cheeks' – and he decided he must write it down and incorporate it in a poem. Monica's boy-friend climbed out of the driver's seat and called to her at the shop doorway, something that mouthed like he was going to park the car and would be back. The boy-friend looked not quite so old as Bernard had thought him to be on the first impression. And that was curiously quenching to his spirits.

Dressed, he took up the phone, to put into action the plan that he had formulated the night before while composing himself for sleep (he had taken a Tuinal capsule, to ensure that his slumbers would not be disturbed by the memory of Garbisian's cyanosed face, nor by thoughts of murderous Bolsheviks). He dialled Alec's home number and presently his brother answered.

'Alec, this is Bernard. Don't say anything, in case we're being overheard. Listen – I'm going home, to Vicarage Gardens, to turn the place inside out for signs of the you know what . . .'

'Oh yes, I get you,' said Alec, who sounded rather down.

'The trouble is going to be Minna. Here's what I want you to do. Telephone Vicarage Gardens immediately and ask Minna – *order* her if she starts acting up – to come round to your place at once. Tell her . . . oh, tell her that the wife isn't well and needs someone to look after her.'

'That wouldn't even be an excuse,' said Alec glumly. 'Ekaterina's not herself this morning. I'm really quite worried for her.'

'*Who* did you say?' asked Bernard, thinking he had not heard aright.

'Ekaterina,' replied Alec. 'Kitty's decided to be called Ekaterina from now on. I'm really quite worried about the way she's acting.'

'I'm not surprised,' said Bernard unfeelingly. 'Look, it's nine o'clock now. If you don't phone me back before nine-thirty, I shall assume that Minna has arrived with you, and I'll go straight round to Vicarage Gardens, okay?'

'All right, Bernard.'

Bernard rang off. As he did so, it occurred to him that it was the first time in his relationship with his elder brother that Alec had ever fallen in with a suggestion –

call it an instruction – that had emanated from him. He was pondering on this when the phone rang. He picked it up.

'Bernard, it's me.' His other brother, James.

'I've been meaning to ring you, James. It's a shame about Father.'

'Yes,' said James doubtfully. 'Er, look, Bernard, I wonder if I can talk to you some time. This morning, for instance.'

'Sorry, but I've got a lot to do this morning – things connected with Father's affairs, you know.'

'Oh, I see. Yes, of course.' He sounded doubtful. And something else – worried? 'I say, Bernard, is everything all right, old chap?'

'What do you mean, "all right"?' demanded Bernard, suffering a sudden small pang of unease.

A pause.

'Well, I don't quite know, really. I suppose I'm rather confused by the way things have happened so suddenly – Father's death and all that. Bernard – if there's anything I can do, anything at all, you will contact me immediately, won't you?'

'Of course.'

'So long then.'

'So long, James.'

He put down the receiver. Now that was very odd. Here was his second senior brother, also hanging on his words and waiting for orders. Admittedly, James had never been anything like so overbearing as Alec, but he possessed an equally pushy wife, and that amounted to almost the same thing. What had come over them both, his brothers? Could it be that, now Father was gone, a curious rift in the structure of the family relationship was turning them towards their formerly despised young brother for leadership?

He pondered over this till nine-thirty, then left the flat.

Monica was at the shop door as soon as he appeared, almost as if she had been waiting for him. She barred his way, coming even closer than was her habit, so that her perfume — atomized by the warmth of her body, in defiance of the chill wind that blew up Scunthorpe High Street — met his nostrils in a shock-wave.

'I'm so sorry to hear about your father,' she said, gusting at him peppermint-flavoured toothpaste in competition with her perfume. 'Saw it in last night's evening paper. Please accept my sincere sympathy at your sad loss.'

'Thank you very much,' said Bernard.

'I hope he didn't suffer,' she said.

'He passed away in his sleep,' said Bernard.

'What a blessing. What a lovely way to go.' She moistened her lips and made a small fluttering gesture with her hands towards a tall figure that loomed from the shop doorway behind her. 'This is my friend, Mr Chuck Waller. Chuck, meet Mr Davis, who lives in the flat above, and whose father passed away very suddenly yesterday.'

'Hi, there.' Chuck Waller in close-up looked like a middle-aged cowboy extra in a Western movie. He was dressed in a rubberized trenchcoat with epaulettes, wrist straps and leather buttons, and his pale blue eyes seemed to peer from afar. 'Sure sorry to hear about your loss, sir.'

They shook hands. 'From the States?' ventured Bernard.

'Canadian,' replied Waller.

'Got to go,' said Bernard, adding lamely, 'got to fix my father's affairs.'

'I stopped the milk till Monday, like you asked me,' Monica fluttered at him. 'But if you want a couple of pints to see you over the weekend . . .'

'I'll be fine, thanks,' said Bernard. 'Goodbye, Mr Waller. Goodbye, er . . .'

He ducked his head and walked quickly up the street towards the intersection that led to the back street where the Aston was parked. To his relief, it was still there. Still – as far as he could make out – acting as hearse to the remains of the Armenian; he peered into the back and checked that the humped form under the blanket and the dirty linen looked untidy, merely. Straightening up, he met the regarding eyes of the Chinese behind the steamed-up kitchen window of the Cathay Flower. They waved and grinned, and he nodded and waved back to them.

No need to take the car the three blocks to Vicarage Gardens; in any event, he did not fancy the idea. Let Garbisian stay where he was till nightfall.

Vicarage Gardens is a discreet and tree-lined thoroughfare off the main, south-bound road, with the town museum on one corner. The houses in it are large, well-constructed and mostly dating from the early part of the century. The Davis family had settled there in Bernard's infancy, and he had lived there – apart from four years away at one of the excellent public schools that proliferate in rural Leicestershire and what used to be Rutland – till he had moved into the High Street flat after his mother's death, when Minna Hodge had begun to supplement her housekeeping duties by occasional forays into the old man's bed.

The Davis family had never been a neighbourly lot, but Bernard was touched to see that the two houses flanking, and the ones opposite, had their blinds and curtains drawn as a mark of respect to the dead.

He went up the drive and quietly let himself in the front door with his latchkey.

And knew, or sensed, immediately that something was wrong!

The wide hallway was in deep shadow, for the curtains were drawn at the windows each side of the door and on the landing above. Closed, also, were the room doors leading off.

'Are you there, Minna?' he called out.

No answer.

But he had certainly heard something: someone had moved in the house immediately after he had quietly closed the door behind him. And that person was upstairs.

'Minna!' he tried again.

Silence.

The hall telephone stood on the windowsill close by his hand. He had an impulse – instantly quenched – to dial 999 for the police. What about getting Alec? Not a good idea! James? Even less good! He caught his reflection in the hat-stand mirror, and squared his shoulders to fit the image of the new Bernard Davis.

There was an umbrella-stand by the door. In addition to all else, it held a knobbly-topped walking-stick. Bernard lifted it out and hefted it, tapping the knob in the palm of his hand. Still tapping silently, he began to tiptoe upstairs.

Long experience – dating from the times when he had

crept down in the night to raid the pantry for bread-and-jam – reminded him that the third step from the top had a loud and treacherous creak; this he avoided by stepping right over it. And so, he reached the upper landing.

And saw that the door to his father's bedroom was ajar. All the others were closed.

He moved slowly towards his father's room. Half-a-dozen silent steps brought him there. As his hand went out to touch the door, and it yielded slightly to his finger-tips, he caught again the languid scent of the arum lilies. He pushed the door further open – and saw nothing.

The tall candles at the bed were no longer lit. The room was in darkness; only a faint loom of muffled daylight at the far end betrayed the presence of the heavily-draped windows.

He felt for the light switch on the right of the door and depressed it. Nothing happened – the room remained dark.

The shaft of the walking-stick felt slippery with his own sweat, as he lifted it up and held the sharper end away from him, pointing it like a probe. Probing still, he walked slowly into the room, towards the windows.

He counted the paces by the ticking of a vein in his temple. Five paces brought him abreast of the bed; his right trouser leg brushed against its edge. He paused when his foot came down upon something; something that squashed beneath his tread. Stooping, he picked it up; felt a moistness on his fingers; that, and a sudden bursting of scent buds. He was holding the broken head of an arum lily from one of the tall vases.

Who had extinguished the candles? And who despoiled the death flowers?

One – two – three more paces brought him to the

windows. He reached and dragged aside the velvet drapes, and his eyes were dazzled by winter's sudden daylight that swept the room.

He turned and looked back the way he had come, from the opened door, taking in the deathbed. And he gave a cry of shocked horror.

The chapelle ardente had been violated!

The candlesticks overturned; the tall vases thrown aside and their contents trampled and scattered; worse, the bed had been despoiled: sheets, pillows pulled to the floor, and a great rent torn down the middle of the mattress, so that its stuffing and springs hung out like bared entrails.

He moved quickly over and stood by the bed, staring down at it, mind racing.

What had the obscene vandals done with Father's body?

By now, his eyes were recovering from their sudden translation from near darkness to blinding daylight; the areas of part-blindness were fading away and his vision clearing.

And from out of the corner of one eye, he saw that he was not alone in the room!

Slowly, he turned, raising his makeshift cudgel as he did so. It made hardly a sound on the thickly-carpeted floor – as his nerveless fingers sprang convulsively open and dropped it. The scream that rose to his lips died with the effort.

In an armchair by the dressing-table, facing him, with huge hands spread out and bare feet splayed below the old-fashioned striped woollen nightshirt, sat Prince Vladimir Ilich Davydov, yclept Vernon Davis. The pennies had fallen from his sloping, Tartar eyes, and they stared out from the sabre-cut, livid and high-cheekboned face with an expression of angry loathing. A fitful winter's sunbeam gleamed from a bared, stainless steel tooth at a corner of the thin-lipped mouth. In death – as in life – he was all fury.

The door creaked on its hinges . . .

Bernard's head flicked round. Closing again, the door revealed the figure crouched behind it. Five feet and a bit, and a levelled pistol.

'Good God! How did you get in here?' cried Bernard.

Casimir Podolski pushed the door closed with the toe of his boot. The pale eyes told nothing, but Bernard's own state of panic enabled him to detect a fellow-sufferer; the Pole was terrified. His mouth was the give-away.

'Bernard, are you armed?' demanded the other.

'Of – of course not!' Bernard blurted. Then, his sense of propriety reasserting itself. 'Put that damned thing down, man. Don't you have any respect for the dead?'

At this, the Pole's face crumpled. The cynical mouth quivered and broke. Lowering the pistol, he pressed his other hand to his eyes and began to sob loudly.

'It must be found!' he wailed, choking on the words. 'If you have it, you must give it to me, Bernard! They are coming . . . we shall suffer . . . we shall all suffer!'

'Who are coming?' cried Bernard.

'The Soviets!' Podolski lowered his hand and stared at the other with streaming eyes. 'They know all about thing that your father brought from Ukraine. To get it, they will do anything . . . anything!'

(Anything! A division of crack infantry, etcetera, etcetera!)

'How do *you* know this, Casim?' demanded Bernard accusingly.

The Pole lowered his head in slack defeat.

'After war was over,' he said brokenly, 'I return to Poland. Soviets arrest me and give me interrogation. They want to know where I have been in England, who are my friends. When they hear that I know your father, they make a deal. My mother will be safe in Poland if I go back to England and resume friendship with man who was formerly known as Prince Davydov.'

'You – you mean you've spied on us all these years!' cried Bernard. 'You've accepted our hospitality – ' he pointed indignantly to the figure in the chair – 'played chess with Father every Wednesday evening – and reported all our doings to the damned Bolsheviks!'

A pallid ghost of his old cynicism played at the corners of the Pole's lips. 'In twenty-seven years, I have reported nothing,' he said. 'Soviets were not interested in doings of the old undertaker of Scunthorpe. It has been a sinecure for me. I have enjoyed freedom of the West. My old mother died in peace – may God rest her soul. All has been bland and harmless. But now . . .' His pale eyes flared with terror.

'*What* now?' snarled Bernard. 'What happened to upset your cosy little sinecure?'

The Pole took a pace towards him, his empty hand clutching at Bernard's sleeve.

'The thing that your father brought from Ukraine,' he wailed, 'they must have it back. Do not think you will ever be allowed to keep it, now that they know. Give it to me, Bernard. I will return it to them when they come, and it will save your life . . . and mine!'

Bernard shook off his grasp angrily. He gestured round

the room, taking in the scattered bedclothes, the upset vases and trampled lilies, the disembowelled mattress, the corpse.

'You had a bloody good hunt for it, didn't you?' he shouted. 'You earned your forty pieces of silver all right this morning, you bastard! But you didn't find what you were looking for. And I'll tell you this, man – ' he took the Pole by the shoulders and shook him, so that the pistol fell, unregarded, to the floor – 'you aren't *going* to find it – not if I can help it!'

The Pole was quite unresisting. When Bernard unhanded him, he straightened his coat with a gesture of simple dignity, but made no attempt to retrieve the pistol.

He said quietly: 'Then we are both dead men, my dear Bernard. For when they come here, they will kill you to silence you, and they will kill me because I lied to them for twenty-eight years about your father.'

'What lies did you tell them about him?' growled Bernard.

'I let them go on believing that he was who he claimed to be,' said the other.

'But . . .'

'No, my dear Bernard. Your father was not the former Prince Davydov. He was an impostor!'

They went down to the drawing-room. Before that, Bernard had insisted on returning the *chapelle ardente* to something like its former order, by tidying the bed, replacing vases and candlesticks, relighting candles. And reverently carrying the corpse back to its bier.

Down in the drawing-room, Bernard poured a stiff vodka for the Pole and three fingers of whisky for himself.

'Right, Casimir,' he said. 'Start talking.'

'I knew real Prince Davydov,' said the Pole. 'Only from afar, you understand. He was arrogant young pig, and master of all the lands about the village where we lived. Once I saw him present my older brother with prize at local gymnasium. He was not a man who was easy to impersonate, for, you see, though officer in Imperial Guards, he only had one arm. The left arm he lost after hunting accident, and he had empty left sleeve.'

'Oh!' exclaimed Bernard. He had been assembling arguments about how it would be impossible to disprove identity after the passing of — it must have been fifty-five years. A man changes a lot in fifty-five years; but not all that much. He does not grow an arm.

'So you see?' The Pole shrugged his shoulders in a gesture of hopelessness.

'But they'll never know now,' said Bernard. 'Father's dead, and will be buried on Tuesday. How will they know you've been lying to them all this time?'

'I cannot take the chance,' said Podolski. 'Those who come will be well-briefed. They will have description of true prince, perhaps even photographs taken before Revolution. They have only to see body — and they will see body, make no mistake, my dear Bernard, for they will search everywhere — or ask questions around the town, and they will know I have lied!' He downed his vodka in one gulp.

A score of questions teemed in Bernard's mind. One had to be asked.

'Who was my father,' he demanded, 'if not Prince Davydov?'

The Pole shrugged his shoulders and pouted his lower lip.

'He never betrayed that to me,' he said. 'And I never gave him slightest suspicion that I knew his secret. For twenty-eight years I enjoyed his friendship – oh yes, my dear Bernard, he was not easy man, your father, but I had genuine affection for him – and Soviets gave neither of us any trouble. Till last June . . .'

'And what happened last June to change all that?'

Podolski held out his glass as Bernard proffered the vodka bottle. 'Last June,' he said, 'I realize that your father is being followed. I nearly shoot myself, because I think that Soviets have imported another agent, who will discover deception, and that all will soon be finished for me. But I decide to wait a little longer – meanwhile, I report to Moscow that Prince Davydov is being followed by another, so that they will know I am keeping my eyes open. And do you know what?'

'Surprise me,' said Bernard wryly. The whisky was beginning to take effect: deadening his screaming nerve-ends.

'The new man is not Soviet agent!' declaimed Podolski dramatically. 'Soviets demand his description, and when I give it to them, they are able to identify him as American agent! Delicious irony! – Moscow gives me commendation and rise in pay!'

'Then what, Casim?'

'After that,' said the Pole, 'Moscow asks for weekly report. Suddenly Prince Davydov and his family become interesting to them. Not only must I report activities of American agent, but I must also tell them of family's comings and goings. Yours included, my dear Bernard.'

'You told them about me going to London on Thursday?' cried Bernard.

The Pole nodded. 'And name of hotel at which you were staying,' he confirmed. 'But I had no idea it was important – how could I? It is not till this morning that I receive signal which tells me about the item that your father brought back from Ukraine . . .'

Bernard interrupted him harshly. 'What *is* this thing, Casim?' he demanded. 'What's its size, shape, dimensions? You call it an item – what sort of item?'

'Bernard, that they have not told me,' said Podolski. 'You must believe me, my dear fellow. I only know its great value is immediately apparent because it is heavily encrusted with jewels. I am ordered to make preliminary search, in case your father died before he was able to conceal it. But, as we have seen . . .' he gave a hopeless gesture in the direction of the floor above.

'And what next?'

'Next, they are sending a party of their best men. These will be experts. Trained investigators. Killers.'

Bernard felt his stomach roll.

'When are they coming?' he asked in a voice that sounded like someone else's.

'Soon,' said Podolski. 'Certainly tomorrow. Possibly even today. They will uncover everything. Discover everything. Of you, I am not sure. Me . . . they will certainly kill.'

It was at that moment that there came a strident ring on the front-door bell. Podolski gave a shrill whimper and sank to his knees, burying his face in his hands.

'I am old man,' he sobbed, 'but I do not want to die!'

The bell rang again. It was followed by a knock. Bernard had an illuminating thought. First checking with his watch, he strode swiftly out of the room, and the Pole watched him go with a wide-eyed, disbelieving stare.

Bernard opened the front door. It was the postman, as he had guessed.

'Registered parcel, sir,' said the man, proffering a stub of indelible pencil. 'Sign please.'

Bernard scrawled his name on a slip and took the package in his hands. With a sense of mild self-congratulation, he observed that his handiwork had survived the overnight mails without so much a scuffing of the corners or a piece of tape coming unstuck. And his father's name and address stared up at him in his own neat handwriting.

'Thank you, sir. Good day.'

Bernard nodded and shut the door. Turning, he saw the Pole leaning weakly against the jamb of the drawing-room doorway, the pistol trailing from his limp hand. Bernard took the weapon from him and slipped it into his own jacket pocket.

'You won't be needing that where you're going,' he said firmly and reassuringly.

'Where *am* I going?' asked Podolski in puzzlement.

'As far as you can go,' said Bernard. 'I would suggest somewhere with a nice climate and a complaisant immigration service. Mexico will fill the bill splendidly, or so I have learned through the medium of fiction.'

'I have no money to run with,' cried the Pole. 'They do not pay me much, the Soviets. Not even with recent rise they give me. In all the world, I do not have more than a hundred pounds, maybe a little less.'

Bernard broke open the brick-shaped parcel, to show the neat bundles of twenty-pound notes lying cosseted within their folds of corrugated card. The Pole's eyes widened with awe.

'There's seven and a half thousand pounds here,

Casim,' Bernard said quietly. 'It's a very small part of the thing my father brought back from the Ukraine – and you can have it.'

'You – you would do this for me, Bernard?' Podolski was beginning to cry again, to Bernard's resumed embarrassment.

'You're welcome to it, Casim,' he said briskly. 'After all, you played square with my old man all those years and didn't blow the whistle on him. I think he'd have approved of you having it. Now, old chap, pull yourself together and disappear before the Bolsheviks come looking for you. If you take my tip, you'll grab a hired car and drive to Leeds airport. With any luck, you could be out of the country by nightfall.'

The Pole took Bernard's hand, his pale eyes brimming with love and gratitude.

'How can you find it in your heart to forgive me, my dear Bernard?' he said brokenly. 'When I think of trouble I have brought upon you.'

'Forget it,' said Bernard briskly. 'My old man brought the trouble when he brought that damned thing – whatever it is – over from the Ukraine. This situation could have blown up at any time during the last fifty-five years. Now it's come – and it's up to me to deal with it the best I can.'

Podolski shook his head in wonderment.

'You are surprising me, Bernard,' he murmured. 'Always I have thought of you as dreamer. Content always to be existing in the great shadow of your father. But now . . .'

Bernard grinned.

'You think I'm coping with the situation rather well?

Yes, I suppose I am. Yes, I suppose I'm quite surprising myself.'

Casimir Podolski had disappeared down tree-lined Vicarage Gardens, on the first leg of an odyssey that might well bring him to an anonymous safety. With him went the seven and a half thousand pounds that should secure his passage to that safety. Bernard watched him go, from an upstairs window, and felt better for it.

Back to the pressing, practical problems . . .

It. The object. The item. The treasure. The thing was certainly not in what should have been the most likely place – which was Father's bedroom. That greatly reduced the probability of it being in the house at all. And was it really feasible to start ripping up floorboards?

A short cut to finding the treasure was even more vital now that he knew the Bolsheviks were closing in. His best option was to know its whereabouts, and to use it as a bargaining counter – perhaps to bargain for his very life. The worse option – and Bernard crossed his legs tightly at the thought, and felt his extremities shrink – was to fall into their hands *before* he could find the thing, and to be 'interrogated.'

How would the new and capable Bernard Davis stand up to torture? Very indifferently, he fancied. It is easy enough to be brave up to one's limit, when one has the comforting retreat of disclosure to fall back on as soon as that limit is reached; but it is a very different matter when one simply is not in a position to deliver the goods; then the first sight of the red-hot pliers would be enough to stop the heart, surely.

Short cuts . . .

How about the old man leaving the thing in a strong box at the bank? Likely – but, since it was Saturday, there was nothing he could do till the bank opened on Monday.

Wait a minute, though – the manager. Ask him! Ask if he knows anything about the old man having a safe deposit!

Bernard riffled through the telephone directory, and found the number of Akers, the bank manager, who lived in nearby Bottesford.

He dialled the number. No reply. Probably out doing the weekend shopping with his wife.

Think again . . .

The solicitors! Father could have left instructions with the family solicitors! Why hadn't he thought of that – the most likely solution – before? They didn't work Saturdays, either, but the senior partner, old man Jacobs, lived only just round the corner. He looked out the number and dialled it. The phone at the other end was picked up almost immediately.

'Hello. Is that Mr Jacobs?'

'Yes. Who's speaking, please?'

'This is Bernard Davis. I wondered if you could help . . .'

'Mr Davis! Oh, may I say how sorry I am about your father's passing? My sincere condolences, sir.'

'Thank you, Mr Jacobs,' said Bernard. 'That's what I'm ringing you about. I know my brother has arranged for the will to be read on Tuesday after the funeral, but I wondered if – it occurred to me – that you might have had some – er – supplementary instructions from my father.'

'Supplementary instructions?' came the rejoinder. 'Do

you mean supplementary instructions concerning your-self, Mr Davis?'

'Yes, that's right.'

'As a matter of fact, I did.'

'You *did*?'

'Why yes, Mr Davis. There is a communication for you from your late father.'

'Can I have it now, Mr Jacobs? You can't imagine how . . .'

'Sir, if I may interrupt you for a moment, to explain the situation. The late Mr Davis senior entrusted me with a letter addressed to yourself, with instructions that I post it to you after his demise.'

'Post it to me?'

'Yes, Mr Davis was quite explicit on that point. I was given written instructions, and to this effect: that I was to post the letter so as to ensure that you did not receive it sooner than four days after his death.'

'Four days? Then . . .'

'He did not specify working days or non-working days, Mr Davis, so – given that he passed away on Friday – I have taken the day in question to be Monday next, the day after tomorrow.'

'Mr Jacobs!' cried Bernard. 'I must have that letter immediately. It's a matter of life or . . .'

'I'm afraid that would be quite out of the question, Mr Davis,' came the solicitor's voice, prim and disapproving. 'Even if it were in my possession, which it no longer is . . .'

'You mean?' cried Bernard.

'I have already posted it,' replied the other. 'In point of fact, I took the dog for a walk after breakfast and caught the early collection. The letter, Mr Davis – your late father's letter to you – is already on its way through the postal system and, since it has gone by first-class mail, must almost certainly reach you by the first delivery on Monday. Is there any other way in which I can be of assistance to you, sir?'

'You – you've no idea what's in that letter?' asked Bernard.

'No, I have not. Your late father did not communicate its contents to me.'

'Thank you, Mr Jacobs.' Bernard put down the receiver and looked at his reflection in the hall mirror. He looked a thousand years old; like Tolland man, dredged up after centuries in a bog. And no wonder. What in heaven's name was he going to look like by the time that letter landed on the mat on Monday morning, after two sleepless nights and two days of living on whisky and fingernails? – always supposing he lived that long; always supposing that the Bolsheviks didn't get him first!

One bright light in all this darkness, though: he had the promise of the letter to give to *them* – if the worst came to the worst.

For one thing was certain: that letter would contain the old man's instructions for him, Bernard, to take possession of the secret treasure, so that the family could continue to benefit as they had done all through the years. As to why Father had stipulated a four-day moratorium on the information: well, that was all of a piece with the old man's sly, perverse nature; nothing would have delighted him more than the thought of the despised Bernard searching high and low and running himself ragged. And if there was any more particular reason, it would probably be revealed in the letter.

His best course now, Bernard decided, was to return

to the flat. Nothing to hold him here now. The dead man upstairs would keep his own counsel till Monday, and meanwhile Minna Hodge would soon be back to watch over him.

Bernard put on his scarf and overcoat, and was just about to open the front door when the telephone rang.

Answer it? Yes – it would probably be Alec.

'My dear Bernard, is it you?' Casimir Podolski – what did *he* want?

'Haven't you gone yet?'

'I am just leaving, when I remember something I should have told you: the name of American agent who appeared on the scene last June. He is still around. His name – Waller.'

'Not – er – Chuck Waller?' demanded Bernard.

'That is him.'

'But he's a boy-friend of the woman who keeps the shop under my flat.'

'Is he? I am not surprised, my dear Bernard. It is quite obvious, from all the activity, that his people have ... *interests*! Goodbye, Bernard. And please be careful.'

CHAPTER VII

Bernard walked quickly, glancing sharply to left and right at every intersection; looking behind him frequently; dying a little every time a car came past him – living the sensation of a hail of machine-gun slugs cutting through his bones and tissues. And a gale-force wind disinterred the last leaves of October from the holes and corners, and sent them whirling above the dark eaves.

There was a police patrol car waiting at the kerb near to his flat, amber warning lights winking. He willed himself not to look towards the two officers inside; fixing his gaze ahead while he passed them and silently screaming to his nerve-ends to be still. As he reached the door, he saw, from the corner of his eye, the two policemen unhurriedly uncoil themselves and get out to come after him.

As he fished for his latchkey, he observed that the boutique was busy with customers: two young girls were working the revolving brassière stand; and Monica craned her head to look over a row of women at the counter. She smiled at him – a tentative, nervous smile, which he did not return.

'Mr Davis, is it, sir – Mr Bernard Davis?'

He fumbled the key and nearly dropped it. Surely they must see fear and guilt written across his brow like the mark of Cain?

'Er – that's right, Officer. Anything I can do?'

'We'd like a word with you if that's convenient.' The speaker was known to him by sight, both of them were familiar faces around the town – local bobbies. Both desperately young, hair too long by half; but competent-looking, with that steady, disconcerting lawman's regard that is the same from Tokyo to Tombstone. One of them – the speaker – fair as a Viking; the other with the dark, intense looks of a rabbinical student.

'Of course,' said Bernard. 'Would you like to come in?'

'Don't mind if we do, sir. A bit chilly out here.'

His fingers trembled so much that he had difficulty in inserting the key – which they surely noticed, and drew their own conclusions about his nervous, guilty state.

Up in the living-room, he switched on the gas fire and

turned to regard them.

'Would you like a drink?'

'No, thank you, sir. We're on duty.'

Bernard looked longingly towards the scotch bottle, jibbed for a moment at the promised ordeal of pouring it out, and finally decided to take the chance.

'Now, gentlemen,' he said calmly. 'What can I do for you?'

'I believe you know a fellow named Garbisian,' said the fair one.

The glass dropped between his fingers and shattered to fragments at his feet. Fortunately, he managed to retain his grip on the scotch bottle. They both helped him to pick up the broken shards, and the dark-haired boy made the observation that there was always one piece, the one from the point of impact, that flew the farthest distance and was generally overlooked – a theory that he went some way to proving by finding a large piece of the glass's base over by the door.

'Sorry about that,' said Bernard, part-grateful for the respite which had given him a few seconds to think. 'What name did you say – Garbisian?'

'That's it, sir. How did they spell it, Arnold?' he asked his colleague.

Arnold consulted his notebook.

'Half a mo', Ron. Here we are: G-a-r-b-i-s-i-a-n.'

'Why, of course,' said Bernard. 'I remember him. He was staying at my hotel in London. We got into conversation in the bar and afterwards had lunch – I may say a very good and boozy lunch, ha, ha – together.' He looked from one to the other of them. 'Why – has anything happened to him?' he asked.

'Yes, sir,' said the fair one, Ron. 'His landlady phoned

in to the Metropolitan police this morning to say that he was missing.'

'Missing?' echoed Bernard, after a moment's silence in which they heard the door of Monica's Boutique below give a musical ting.

'He's a chap of very regular habits, you see, sir,' said Ron. 'Otherwise she wouldn't have been so quick off the mark. She was expecting him back on Friday night, you see, but he didn't turn up. Then, when she rang the hotel this morning, they told her his baggage was still in his room and the bed hadn't been slept in. It was then she got in touch with the police, just to check up, like. In case he'd been in an accident and taken off to hospital, or something.'

Bernard was uncomfortably aware that both pairs of eyes were keenly regarding him.

'And where do I come into it?' he asked, with as much casualness as he could summon up – and it was not much.

'Well, the hotel people were able to tell that a Mr Bernard Davis of Scunthorpe split a lunch bill with Garbisian on the Thursday,' said Ron.

'So the Met. boys asked us to come and see you,' added Arnold. 'In case you could throw any light on the matter.'

Bernard assembled a vision of Garbisian's tortured, dead face under the blanket in his car. And switched it off.

'I only spoke to him the once,' he said truthfully. 'On that Thursday lunchtime. It was just a casual meeting.'

Both young policemen nodded understandingly.

'The Met. boys accepted that possibility,' said Arnold. 'Normally, they wouldn't have asked us to bother you,' said Ron. 'Not at this stage. Not with him only missing for one day. It's not much time to go missing in.'

'Only,' said Arnold, opening his notebook again, 'there was something else . . .'

Bernard's throat suffered a sudden contraction, so that his comment came out as a thin wheeze . . .

'Something else?'

'Yes, sir. Funny coincidence, but the Met. boys already had your name. You'd complained about your car being broken into in London, hadn't you?'

('Complained' was putting it a bit high, but it was a small flaw in the story that couldn't do him any harm.)

'Er – yes.'

'Yes, they had the report,' said Ron. 'And strictly between you and us, they think it's more than a coincidence.'

(More than a coincidence! He knew their next demand: '*Do you mind if we search your vehicle, Mr Davis? And we must warn you that a refusal will result in our obtaining a warrant.*')

'They think there's a connection,' said Arnold, 'between Garbisian striking up an acquaintance with you, and the break-in job on your car.'

Amazed, Bernard registered that they were both smiling at him. Friendly, button-holing smiles. You-and-us-together smiles.

'He's known to the Met. boys, this Garbisian,' said Ron.

'He's a bad lad,' said Arnold.

'You mean? . . .' said Bernard.

They both reassumed their bland, blank, incorruptible police looks.

'It could have been that way, Mr Davis,' said Ron.

'Lucky you weren't carrying a lot of valuable stuff in your car.'

'Just goes to show you've got to be careful who you strike up an acquaintance with nowadays,' said Arnold, adding, with a touch of provincial bias, 'particularly down in London.'

'We won't bother you any longer, Mr Davis,' said Ron, 'since you didn't come across Garbisian after Thursday. Thanks for your co-operation.'

He saw them out of the door and down the stairs.

On an impulse, he said: 'If I think of anything, I mean – if I remember anything that Garbisian said which might be of importance, I'll telephone you.'

'That'll be smashing, Mr Davis,' said Ron, giving him an approving 'thumbs-up' from the bottom of the stairs. 'Cheerio for now.'

'Cheerio.'

He shut the door, leaned back against it, mouth open, panting with the effort that the ordeal had cost him.

Damn the Bolsheviks! . . .

They had tied this on him. He had nearly outwitted them and got away with it, but the heavy hand of coincidence and sheer bloody bad luck had worked against him. Now he was on the police file as a potential victim of whatever racket Garbisian had got up to when he hadn't been exporting cynical little scrubbers to heaven knows where. Give it a couple of days' time – or less – and the search for the missing Armenian would be intensified. Old ground would be worked over again. Someone would put a finger on the now slightly overlooked fact that he hadn't actually reported the break-in; those two nice coppers would be sent back to do a closer re-check on the Aston's broken rear door. He'd be promoted from potential victim to suspect murderer.

'I only hope to God,' he said aloud, 'that we can get Garbisian safely buried and out of the way before then!'

And then, he cried: 'Curse the Bolsheviks! Damn and blast that grubby old German they buried up in Highgate Cemetery – he started it all!'

Two o'clock. The flat above Monica's Boutique he now saw as a fortress: indeed, he had taken all reasonable precautions to make it so: all the windows closed and latched; the window curtains drawn at the back, for they were overlooked by a taller building opposite, from which a marksman could send a well-directed bullet; the door at the top of the stairs double-locked and bolted.

He hoped he was over-dramatizing his situation. The memory of Casimir Podolski's story reminded him he was not; the unaccustomed feel of the Pole's pistol in the damp palm of his hand opened up the unpleasant vista of worlds undreamed of by him, ways of living that he had only known vicariously.

The weapon was a tiny thing; a Biretta, made in Italy – that much he was able to read on it. It was of a type he supposed to be an automatic. Fiddling with it, he found seven very small nickel-plated cartridges lying in a spring-loaded magazine in the handgrip. As to how to operate the weapon, he was entirely in the dark. There was a small catch handily placed near the right thumb, when one held the thing in one's right hand; he was not able to tell which way was 'safe' and which 'fire'. He only hoped that – come the time if and when he had to use the gun in self-defence – he would win the even chance bet and save his life.

Two o'clock. In, say, four hours' time, he would have

to abandon his fortress and make a rendezvous with Alec at the mortuary gate, with the Aston. He had already tried to reach his elder brother by telephone, but had received no reply.

Come to think about it, what about the others – Alec and the rest of the family? Were they in danger, also, from the Bolsheviks? On balance, he thought not – not yet anyhow. Thanks to the London business, they had almost certainly got him pencilled in as the bloke with the knowledge of the treasure; the target for immediate action.

The trip to the mortuary was not going to be much fun. Thank heavens for Scunthorpe's well-lit streets. Not to mention a fast car. And the little pistol.

Heartened, Bernard took another drink – his fourth since Vicarage Gardens.

He fell asleep in an armchair with the half-finished whisky in his hand, and was awakened by the shrilling of the telephone. Night had fallen, and the street lighting came nakedly in through the windows.

It was Alec. He sounded like a man at the end of his tether.

'Bernard – did you find the – you know?'

'No, but I'm on to it. I'll explain when we meet. What time can you get round there?'

'Give me – give me half an hour. That'll be – seven o'clock. I – I think I can make it by them . . .' his voice tailed off.

'What do you mean, you *think* you can make it?' snapped Bernard. 'Alec, what in hell's the matter with you?'

'It – it's Kitty. I mean Ekaterina. I can't get to her.'

'What do you mean, you can't get to her?'

'She's locked herself in the lounge – with the record player.'

'Doing what?'

'Playing the Russian Imperial Anthem over and over again! Full blast! It's nearly driving me mad!'

Bernard drew a deep breath of exasperation. That dotty woman! 'Look, Alec,' he said, 'never mind about your wife and the record player. A good tune never hurt anybody. Just you get over there in half an hour, or we're all in trouble. Right?'

'All right.'

Bernard rang off. Half an hour to wait. Give it twenty-five minutes, enough to allow for a quick walk to the Aston and the short drive up the High Street to Doncaster Road. Better to be a bit late than early; better to have Alec waiting with the yard gate unlocked and open for him to drive straight in.

It suddenly occurred to him that he was hungry, so he took a polony sausage out of the fridge and munched at it with a mouthful of whisky. Still chewing, he went over to his desk and took out his notebook, opening it at the page containing his current poetic fragment.

Distant yet omnipresent music of airy flutes,
Wispy faerie imaginings,
Borne on these wondrous, elf-lit
Blue and gold-hued . . .

It still lacked a last line.

'Good lord!' he exclaimed aloud, with a note of genuine surprise. And again: 'Good lord, did I write that? It seems very remote now.'

He sat down and took out the Biretta. Between mouthfuls of the polony, he came to the conclusion that, on balance, the probability of the 'up' position of the safety catch being the right position for pulling the trigger was the stronger of the two alternatives. But he did not dare to test his theory there and then, for fear of the noise attracting unwanted attention.

At six minutes to seven, Bernard let himself out of the downstairs door and gently clicked the lock behind him. Monica's Boutique was lit up, like the rest of the High Street shops, but the 'Closed' sign hung behind the glass door. He wondered what *she* was up to – her and her Yankee spy . . .

It was bitterly cold and blowing a gale. A few people were scurrying by, heads bowed against the penetrating east wind. There was not much traffic about. With the milled butt of the little pistol nestling comfortably in his right palm, inside his overcoat pocket, he set off at a brisk walk that was nearly a run.

The back street was also well-lit, and the Aston was actually standing under a street lamp, which provided the advantage of a strong shadow within the car – the better to conceal its contents. The window of the Chinese Take-Away was steamed up; he could see the ghostly silhouettes of the industrious Orientals as he slipped into the driving seat and gunned the big 2·9 litre engine into triumphant life.

And then it happened . . .

A large black car, with four white faces looking out at him: it came from behind, slewed across his front, and halted in the middle of the road ahead, broadside on. Three figures leaped out of it and came running towards the Aston.

Bernard jammed the gear lever in reverse, muffed it first time with a noise like a high-speed drill gone berserk, hit it second time and released his foot from the clutch, spinning the wheel as he did so. The sports car rocketed backwards, crossed the street, mounted the far kerb – and struck the wall with a jolt that threw Bernard back in his seat and nearly dislocated his neck.

The three men fanned out and came on. He could not see their faces because the street lights were behind them.

He slammed the car into second gear, over-revving wildly. His putative would-be assailants leapt aside; he felt the jar of something rebounding off his nearside wing and heard a bellow of pain. Then he was speeding on, and already applying the wheel to make the first corner. He flashed across the High Street without looking right or left; but saw the lights of the large black car in his rear mirror as it swayed round the corner in hot pursuit.

A curious calmness now fell upon Bernard Davis, failed Bachelor of Arts of Oxford University and self-declared poet. He found himself unexpectedly possessed of a detached and analytical view of himself and his predicament. It was as if he was directing the hands, the feet and the eyes of Bernard Davis at some considerable remove; as if – given that the circumstances deteriorated – he would be able to relinquish that control as easily as one switched off a television set, and turn his attention to some more pleasant and gainful pastime. Further analysing his reactions, he supposed that the strange sense of aloofness must be a concomitant of a quality that he had never suspected himself of possessing: the quality of courage.

On analysis, it was clearly useless to attempt to go straight to the mortuary; the Aston's tremendous speed and fingertip manœuvrability were only of marginal advantage in a built-up area – given that his pursuers were close behind and trying hard. He took another look to the rear: they were indeed trying very hard, and holding him.

The best solution: to get out of town, on to a long straight stretch where his mount could win time and distance from his slower adversaries; time and distance to double back and still be at the mortuary gates before Alec gave up in despair and went home to his dotty wife.

On a self-assembled road map positioned somewhere behind his retina, Bernard saw the route out of town to the East – the A18 to Brigg – and a detour by way of Hibaldstow village that would bring him back to Scunthorpe by the same road on which he went out. Call it a round trip of, say, twenty miles. Going flat out on the quiet country straights, the Aston could make it in twenty minutes and still not be in hazard of being picked up by the police for speeding in the built-up areas. Let the opposition beat that!

His glance flickered down to the dashboard clock: one minute after seven. Alec would not have long to wait for him.

Eyes front again, and he was just passing the end of Vicarage Gardens (how was the old patriarch faring in his eternal sleep?), with St Lawrence's Church coming up on the right and the traffic lights changing from green to red. He drove his right foot down, taking the intersection with a margin to spare. Would the opposition stop for the lights, which were doomed to be firmly against them?

In the rearview mirror, he saw the large black car cut unhesitatingly out into the middle of the road, cross the red light and zip under the very nose of a large truck that braked to a spinning halt in the middle of the intersection. Karl Marx would have been proud of them!

Over the railway bridge, and a roundabout coming up ahead. He was driving perilously over the speed limit, but the other's lights were becoming tellingly wider apart. The two cars entered the roundabout, nose to tail. But they did not stay that way for long.

Bernard's second line of consciousness registered the sudden and seemingly inexplicable disappearance of the pursuing headlights without assembling enough external evidence to arrive at an explanation. In the three seconds it took for the Aston to negotiate a quadrant of the roundabout, he brought the forefront of his mind to bear upon the problem. It is possible that an element of clairvoyance intruded upon his deliberations, because he was already applying a drastic correction to the steering wheel when he saw the enemy headlights coming at him from the other side of the roundabout.

In defiance of law, custom and good order, they had gone the wrong way round! In order to meet him head-on!

Bernard felt the front traction soften and die under his hands as the Aston went into a speed drift. A dusting of night frost assisted the movement. He applied correction to the steering wheel, but was fast running out of road. The offside front tyre struck the kerb and blew out with a report like a saluting gun. Curiously, it had the effect of steadying the drift. The car travelled fifty yards down the middle of the road in a crabwise slant and then straightened up. Bernard registered three things: one, the other driver had mistimed his turn and was having to make another circuit of the roundabout; two, the Aston had come out on the wrong road; three, he could forget any idea of going for a night steeplechase across country

– his mount was lame, and like to be his ruin unless he abandoned her. And took to the rough. On foot.

But where?

He was heading east. The railway sidings were on his left and Scunthorpe's flame-tipped chimneys stood like warning beacons in the night sky ahead. A line of mean terraced houses slid past on the right. By a street corner, small children swung round a lamp-post on the end of a rope. A white dog came out into the road and barked at the car that rattled past on one bare wheel rim; Bernard swerved to avoid the animal, and the treacherous wheel nearly took him into a spin.

The enemy headlights were showing again: three or four hundred yards behind, but coming up on him fast – now.

The engine was fighting against the drag of the bare rim; he changed down to third gear, but acceleration was agonizingly tardy – like wading through treacle. Time to get out.

To his left, a dark cavern lined with terraced hovels. The directing brain of the new and superior Bernard Davis programmed him to cut his lights and spin the steering wheel. The Aston rolled recklessly and plummeted into the gloom. A hundred yards and five seconds later, it emerged in the moonlight again, in an area of waste ground flanking the railway sidings. There was a row of tin sheds and a jumble of wrecked cars. Pointing the Aston towards one of the sheds whose doors hung drunkenly open, Bernard switched off the engine. They glided into the darkness with no more sound than the grating of the bare wheel rim on the hard-packed slum earth. He leapt out and securely locked the car doors. No such appointments graced the doors of the shed; he had to be content with a heavy billet of wood to hold them shut.

He looked back the way he had driven. There was a distant jangle of pop music coming from somewhere in the maze of dark hovels, which were thrown into silhouette by the lines of lights in the streets beyond. Nothing moved.

His safest way – or so it seemed to him – lay across the waste ground and over a fence that would bring him on to the main road leading back into the town centre. The Aston – and Garbisian's body – he would have to leave to fate for the time being. The Armenian's remains were doomed to yet another night of uneasy repose. And no telling what the morning would bring.

Bernard set off, moving swiftly over towards the shadowy end of the nearest terrace. There he paused, one hand resting against the grimy brickwork, listening. There was a distant clatter of a dustbin lid, and a cat's harsh yowl.

The ends of three more terraced streets separated him from a couple of hundred yards of sloping scrubland, beyond which were the bright lights of the road and the heavy lorries hurtling up from the South. He peered round the corner of the wall, into the street down which he had driven. Nothing there. Taking a deep breath, Bernard ran quickly across to the next patch of shadow.

A shout followed him!

He heard the clatter of booted feet on cobblestones – and he kept running. Another shout, and a tall figure in broad-brimmed hat and long mackintosh spun into view round the side of the next terrace ahead. The man was holding something. Twenty yards separated them, as Bernard dug into his right-hand pocket and brought out the Biretta. In a frozen instant of time, he saw his adversary stare at him irresolutely and then raise the thing that he was holding. Bernard did likewise, thumbing the safety catch to the upward position as he had planned to do.

A sudden glare of light blinded Bernard, so that his eyes were closed when he squeezed the trigger.

Nothing happened: the Biretta remained obstinately silent. He reversed the position of the safety catch and tried again.

No result. When he opened his eyes the other had doused his flashlamp and was ducking back round the corner. Here was a man who did not intend to wait around while Bernard Davis learned to fire an automatic.

He heard more footfalls behind him!

There was a dark entry leading into the heart of the terrace: the access to the backs of the two rows of houses, with their forest of TV aerials and washing lines. It promised concealment in its secret maze, and Bernard accepted the offer. Pocketing the pistol (what had gone wrong with it?), he set off into the darkness, holding out one hand before him. He had not gone far before the running footsteps went past the end of the entry behind him, and he heard a voice raised in a harsh note of interrogation and another answering flatly.

They had lost him!

It seemed likely that narrow gully would continue the length of the terrace and give him egress to the road at the far end. If not, he had run himself into a trap, a rabbit warren with only one way in and out. And might they not now be waiting for him at the end of the entry, only hesitating to follow him in because they now knew — and it must have been a shock to that fellow to see a gun being aimed at him in his torchlight – that he was armed?

He progressed slowly, probing before him, running a hand along the brickwork of the low wall that contained the mean back yards of the little houses. There were only thin chinks of muted brightness around the edge of some of the curtained back windows. From almost every house came the sound of a Saturday evening TV show. It was seven-thirty and proletarian Scunthorpe was settling down to its blissful hour of Kung Fu.

But not quite all of proletarian Scunthorpe . . .

Bernard's extended hand touched something warm and yielding. The contact drew forth a shrill squeal of alarm.

'*Eeeeh! Gerroff!*' A girl's voice.

'Wassup then?' A youth.

Someone probed at him. The girl cried out again. Bernard felt his arm taken in the grip of someone palpably stronger and physically more adept than he.

'Issa bloody bloke! Hey, what you doin' 'ere?'

'Peepin' Tom!' cried the girl.

'Ah'll give 'im bloody Peepin' Tom!'

A fist came out of the blackness and took Bernard on the arch of his rib-cage just to one side of the sternum, driving the air from his lungs in an agonizing gust and doubling him over in retching helplessness; another punch to the side of the head had him reeling against the wall, where he began to sink to his knees, with everything slipping very far away.

'Dutty old devil!' shrieked the girl. ''E touched me!'

They had a torch on him now. He could see their extremities below the loom of the light: clog-soled platform shoes and a pair of denim legs that ended with bovver boots. One of the boots was already drawn back to kick his head when it touched the ground, and he was sharply, hideously aware of the peril.

But beyond and above the tangible hazards there intruded another and more pressing dread. It was almost immediately realized. From down the far end of the entry, he heard *them* coming at the run.

They would find him lying unconscious under the boot of the outraged young swain!

They would not! – declared the new and superior Bernard Davis.

He clawed at the capping of the wall and straightened himself up, sliding his hand till he felt the latch of the gate that the couple had been leaning against. He had noticed it briefly in the torchlight.

The youth cursed, and made a grab at him; but Bernard was through the gate and staggering towards the back door of the mean house before his tormentor could establish his grip. He fell over a bucket and clattered it before him, so that he and the bucket struck the door together. Next instant, he sprawled over the threshold and into a darkness that smelt of stale soapy water and brussels sprouts. He kicked the door shut behind him and went on his way.

An elderly couple, man and wife, looked round from the flickering image on the TV screen when Bernard Davis burst in from their scullery and leapt across the living-room without a word of greeting. When he had gone, they turned back resignedly to their Kung Fu.

Bernard slammed out of the front door and into the street, to see two figures racing down the terrace towards him from the railway end. He set off at a run in the opposite direction, but had not gone more than a few paces before an acute shortness of breath revealed the full extent of the damage which the youth's body-punch had wrought upon his middle-aged constitution. He was beaten. He would never be able to last fifty yards, and his pursuers were coming up fast.

Bernard set his sights on the end of the dark street. That was the sum of his ambition, now: to take whatever was coming to him in the brightness of the main street lights, out of the shadows.

Ten yards to go – and a yellow car slid into view at the end of the road, and stood there, engine pulsating. A hand came out and pushed wide the passenger's door.

A voice called to him:

'Get in – quickly!' A woman's voice.

Dazzled by the sudden lights, vision clouded with fatigue, he felt rather than saw his way into the yellow car. The driver reached across in front of him and slammed the door. It was hardly done before a jolting start-off bounced Bernard back in his seat.

It was quite a few moments before he had his breath under control to be able to raise his head and look about him.

His chauffeur was concentrating on her task, face set and fixed firmly ahead. Dark glasses hid her eyes, and a pulled-down beret her hair.

'Who – who are you?' croaked Bernard.

The young woman threw him a swift glance and flashed a very white-toothed smile.

'I thought you'd recognized me on the motorway yesterday,' she said. 'I'm by way of having become your guardian angel.' And she pulled off the beret and shook her mane of crisp, blonde hair.

'Janice!' cried Bernard.

She was the massage-girl from London!

CHAPTER VIII

She knew about the available parking space behind the flat, and they left her yellow Fiat in the Aston's usual spot outside the Cathay Flower. The east wind had brought a feathering of sleet to the night air, and she took Bernard's hand and urged him to run with her; they sped up the street together, and the Chinese stopped work for a few moments and watched through the window after them, almond eyes wistful. They ran all the way, through the sleet, hand-in-hand, stepping like stately dancers in a speeded-up pavan.

The door of the flat closed behind them, bolted and double-locked, he turned to her.

'Thanks for what you did,' he said. 'I think, if you hadn't come along, that those chaps would have done for me.'

She took off her beret and picked off a glassy shard of sleet between finger and thumb, examining it with interest.

'The Soviets wouldn't have killed you,' she said flatly. 'Not there and then. They want information from you, and I happen to know they've got a dinky little torture chamber already fitted up in the cottage that they've taken on the Doncaster road. That's where you'd be by now.' Her large blue eyes twinkled humorously at him over the tops of her fingers.

Bernard swallowed hard. 'I had a blessed gun with me,' he said, 'but it failed me in the emergency.'

'Show me,' said Janice.

He handed her the Biretta. She took it in her right hand and snapped back the upper part of its body with her left. Click, snap. He saw a nickel-jacketed cartridge bolt like a rabbit down a hole.

'You didn't cock it, you twit,' she said mildly. 'Which means there wasn't a shell up the spout, so you could have gone on pulling away at the trigger for ever.'

'I know nothing about guns,' confessed Bernard.

'It's a woman's gun, anyhow,' said Janice. 'I'll hang on to it.' She slipped the Biretta into the pocket of her black leather coat.

'You're enormously capable,' he said wistfully.

'That's what you pay your taxes for.' She smiled – that girl-in-the-holiday-brochure smile which started a yearning tug at his heart for all he'd never known; for lost youth, lost opportunities.

To cover his confusion, he said: 'How long have you been my capable guardian angel, then?'

'I was assigned to you when you arrived in London,' she said. 'Our people had already moved into the room next to yours and connected with your phone.'

'Who are – your people?'

'Internal Security. Nothing to do with any similar organization. No connection with the police. Nothing.'

'Why me?'

'Because you were being trailed by almost everyone in town except the Boy Scouts and the League of Fallen Women. We decided to move in close and see what – if anything – you were carrying that was so hot. It was a golden opportunity when we intercepted your phone call to the massage service.'

He felt a hot flush of embarrassment rise from his

shirt collar, pass his ears and encompass his whole countenance.

'It's – it's a thing I've never done before,' he murmured hoarsely.

'That was pretty obvious,' she said. 'And it was a new departure for me, too – unless you count the time I was called upon to massage bruised shins in the changing-room after school hockey.'

Covering his confusion with civility, he said: 'Would you like a drink?'

'This time, I'll say yes,' she smiled.

He busied himself with the glasses, and said: 'So you moved in close, searched my belongings and discovered I was carrying nothing interesting. What then?'

'We got orders to back away for a while and leave everybody plenty of opportunity to manœuvre,' she said. 'And it certainly worked. It was as if the sky fell in the following morning. Your very good health. Here's to lady masseuses everywhere.'

'Cheers,' said Bernard, raising his glass. 'And here's to you.'

'After the Soviets rubbed out Garbisian,' she said, 'what did they do with his body – dump it on you?'

'Yes!' he exclaimed. 'All strangled and blue – horrible!'

'Garbisian worked for the Americans,' said Janice. 'Like that other useless clot Waller. You know, espionage offers some of the opportunities of acting: given the right sort of part, you can pad it out to a degree that you're practically taking over the lead. Garbisian and Waller have been up to the same game. They took simple routine surveillance and blew it up into the big time. And look where it got Garbisian.'

'He's in the back of my Aston Martin,' said Bernard, and he told her how he had left it in the shed on the waste ground.

'You can put your mind at rest about the body,' she told him. 'My people will take over and dispose of that. There's to be no reference to the civil authority. The police will never know.'

'God, what a relief!' exclaimed Bernard. What a wonderful, wonderful girl she was. Pride and joy of the School Hockey First XI, he didn't doubt for a moment – and grown up into a big, buxom, bouncing, blue-eyed, all-British beauty. 'Have another drink!' he cried.

Half an hour later, he decided that Alec would have given up hope of seeing him at the mortuary and have gone back home. He picked up the telephone to ring his elder brother. The line was dead.

Janice listened also. 'It's been cut,' she said calmly. 'The Soviets are making sure you're incommunicado. When they've got you good and worried, they'll maybe ring up and propose a deal.'

'But – I don't have anything to make a deal with!' wailed Bernard.

Janice slowly put down the receiver. Her fine eyes were clouded with doubt. She seemed to hesitate, looking down at her shapely fingers. And then, she said: 'I don't want to be pushy, but I have to tell you that we know that the Russians are after something in your possession. And that they'll . . .'

'Move heaven and earth to get it!' supplied Bernard. 'Right! But it so happens that I don't have the bloody thing, my dear young lady. What's more, I don't know what it is, either – only that it's of enormous intrinsic value. But I *may* know more on Monday morning.'

Her blue eyes flared at him.

'Monday morning?'

Then he told her. And when he had finished, she stood up and took off her black leather coat.

'Very well,' she said briskly. 'Nothing remains but for me to stay here and continue to be your guardian angel till the mail arrives on Monday a.m.'

Underneath the coat, she wore black ski pants and a black sweater that looked as if it had been smoothed on to her splendid torso with a palette knife while in a semi-liquid state. She reached her arms up and stretched luxuriantly. Bernard swallowed and dropped his gaze.

'What then?' he asked huskily.

'I'm afraid it'll have to be turned over to us for a start,' she said. 'Afterwards, the Crown might graciously allow you to keep it under the due processes of the law of treasure trove. In any event, you'll be protected from the Soviets, you and your family. So you've nothing to worry about. Well, looks as if you're going to have to put up with me for a whole day, not to mention two nights. Do you play poker?'

'I don't play card games at all.'

'Got a TV?'

'No.'

'Radio?'

'It's broken.'

Hands on hips, eyes flaring, she stared down at him: every inch the pride of the School First XI Hockey grown to triumphant British womanhood.

'Well, what *do* you do with your spare time?' she demanded.

This, he knew with a clear and burning light, was the

moment to speak out. This, the cue that would have brought the sardonic smile and the voluptuous, drooping eyelid from the new Bernard Davis whose brief and promising career had fizzled out so dolefully on their last meeting.

Or take Garbisian (when alive): not all his flabby avoirdupois, nor his dyed hair and moustaches, nor his advanced years and alien blood, would have inhibited him for one moment from giving the true voluptuary's reply to this delicious girl's taunting question. *Encore de l'audace! Et toujours de l'audace!*

She was tapping her foot impatiently now (such a small, but capable-looking foot, encased in shapely suède après-ski boots), and looking down at him with a coquetry that was beginning to shade off into exasperation.

'I'll put it another way,' she said. 'How are we going to pass the time, cooped up in this poky little flat from now till Monday morning?'

'I – I suppose you wouldn't be interested in reading my poetry?' faltered Bernard.

At eleven o'clock they sat down to a supper that she had composed from the residuals of the fridge: eggs, sausage, two rashers of bacon, a hunk of old cheese; half a bottle of tolerable hock. She ate with his poetry notebook propped against the wine bottle in front of her.

Bernard's head was bowed over his plate, and he was smarting with resentment. Her criticisms had been sand-blasting his ego throughout the preparation of the meal – a process which had been greatly protracted by their progression half-way down a bottle of scotch. The conjunction of the culinary and the poetic arts, well seasoned with alcohol, seemed to have a deleterious effect upon his companion's mild and reasonable air. She was being, he thought, extremely acidulous about his pieces, and verging on the downright rude.

'All this airy-fairy nonsense,' she said, spearing a sausage with all the devastating expertise of a pig-sticker in the glorious days of the Raj, 'all this greenery-yallery insistence on art for art's sake. There's no such thing as art for art's sake. Each class in our society has its own artistic criteria. You're a pampered middle-aged man who's never had to do a hand's turn, who's been feather-bedded from the hard knocks of life since the day he was born. Hence your artistic criteria: formalism, abstraction, hedonism, and a romantic decadence that looks back to other days – days that can never return. Outside of your cosy cocoon there are things like misery and despair, hunger, struggle, sweat, aspiration – things that help to make up the sum of human experience, things that might just as well not exist as far as you're concerned.'

'I am concerned with these things,' said Bernard, as calmly as he was able, 'but they're artistically irrelevant to me. True, I've never had to struggle for my existence, nor have I ever been hungry. On the other hand, I've known a little misery and quite a lot of despair. Aspiration has not entirely passed me by, but at my age one learns to accept that aspirations become burdens that can be shed with some relief. All this has nothing to do with art, which transcends the human state, and is forever renewed by the disinterested efforts of succeeding generations of artists, big and small. I am a small artist.'

She took a long pull of her hock. 'You are,' she said flatly. 'A very small artist. They don't come much smaller.'

Ignoring that, he said: 'I'm the sort of small artist

who looks upon the vast pantheon of our common European heritage as a sacred trust. Something to be protected from the incursions of the barbarians who are all round us; something to be loved and cherished. I don't aspire to add to its volume by so much as a pennyweight, but just to take out some of its fine old tunes from time to time and score them for my penny whistle. And mostly for my own amusement. Is that bad?'

Janice exhaled heavily through her finely-wrought nostrils.

'You prove my point out of your own lips,' she said. 'Your view of art is geared to your position in society, which is that of a parasite. Your art is similarly parasitical, self-indulgent, formalistic. What you would call art for art's sake. But it's really for *your* sake. Do you know, I really do think I'm rather drunk? Shall we skip the metaphysics and turn in?'

'It was a very nice meal,' said Bernard lamely.

'I'm the best short-order cook in the business,' she said, gathering up the plates. 'Would you like to turn off the lights and peek through the side of the curtains?'

Mystified, he obeyed her. It was still blowing hard, as evidenced by the occasional pieces of paper, dry leaves, and indefinable scraps of urban flotsam that came bowling up the empty High Street.

Empty, that is, save for the watcher in the shop doorway opposite: a tall figure in a long, rubberized mackintosh and broad-brimmed hat, whose invisible eyes seemed to be directed up to the windows of the flat over Monica's Boutique.

Bernard felt the soft touch of her body against his elbow, and the tang of her scent, as she moved up beside him and looked out also.

'He looks like one of the chaps who came after me,' he said. 'The one I tried to take a shot at.'

'He's just there for window-dressing,' she said. 'To make you jumpy. They don't need to keep so close a tail. When nothing develops tomorrow, they'll stop crowding you.'

'To give me the opportunity to manœuvre?' suggested Bernard.

'You're beginning to get the hang of this game,' she smiled, straightening the curtain again and shutting out the December night. 'I think I'd like a bath. Will that be all right?'

'There's plenty of hot water,' said Bernard. 'And I'll give you a towel. While you're in the bathroom, I'll get my things out of the bedroom and make up a bed on the sofa. I think you'll find the bed quite comfortable. It's double-sized. I'm a restless sleeper.'

Was it his imagination, or did she pause in her movement across the room and throw him a swift, amused glance? Bernard's back was half-turned towards her, on his way to the airing cupboard for a clean towel and sheets. Nothing on earth would have persuaded him to look round and confirm his impression.

She called to him from the bathroom: 'I'm sorry I was rude about your poetry. 'Fraid I haven't entirely outgrown my pink liberal phase that I picked up as a student, when it seemed that it only needed one little shove on everyone's part to turn society into a heaven on earth. How do you work this old geyser?'

'Coming,' said Bernard.

She had taken off her boots and was standing on the bath mat, looking in dismay at his antiquated hot-water heater. Bootless, she was much smaller, reaching only to his chin. He showed her how to work the thing, and she got it right first time. He laid the towel on the rail and left her.

A stiff drink — that was it. He was just at the right degree of insobriety to make a fool of himself with this cool and competent young civil servant lady. She probably had karate, aikido, and all the rest. A splendid culmination to a lifetime of celibacy that would be: to have his collar-bone broken by being thrown across his own living-room.

One more very stiff one — then straight to bed.

Bernard was curled up on the sofa, with only one small wall light burning, and his face turned away from the bathroom door when she came out.

'Are you asleep?' she asked.

'No,' he said.

'I have to read myself to sleep always,' she said. 'Do you have anything?'

'I have a small, but representative, library in the bedroom,' said Bernard. He spoke carefully, subscribing as he did to the fairly common illusion that it was only by his enunciation that he betrayed inebriation. 'As befits a poet and general *littérateur*,' he added.

'I'm sure you have. Good night.'

'Good night.'

The bedroom door shut. He counted the lines of weaving (warp? weft?) on the material of the sofa an inch from his nose. Arriving at thirteen, he lost count and started again. He supposed by now that she would be in bed. And that was a relief. Saved from the consequences of his own folly!

His mind went back to the many follies of his past: to the night of the commemoration ball and to Felicity's good right-hander. Shudderingly, he recalled also an incident that had occurred during one of his London trips in his early thirties; this before the days of the so-called permissive society (whose much-extolled delights had manifestly not come *his* way), when everything was cash on the nail and the drabs were strung out along Piccadilly like coloured beads. Bernard's habitual mien of nervous probity usually served to protect him from the advances of these unfortunate creatures, who had no time to waste on mice when rabbits abounded; but in this instance he had lunched rather well with the editor of a publishing firm who had so far responded to Bernard's hospitality as to intimate that his people might consider publishing Bernard's novel, at Bernard's expense; and it was while he was strolling past Burlington Arcade, and smiling at the memory of his triumph, that the highly-priced lady whose beat lay by that desirable piece of real estate made a certain suggestion to the young *littérateur*.

Completely taken aback, and with his thoughts entirely immersed in the entrancing details of his possible publishing venture, Bernard had blurted out the declaration that was running through his mind; a declaration that, slightly misheard and totally misinterpreted by the daughter of joy, had reduced her first to incredulity, second to mirth, and third to the need to communicate her experience to another of her sort. Bernard remembered how he had fled up Burlington Arcade – past all the elegant boutiques with their choice bibelots, past the horrified stares of the well-heeled *flâneurs* – with the raucous, gin-honed voice of the drab echoing down the glassy vault to her fellow magdalen who graced the beat at the far end:

'*A right one 'ere, Liz! Can you 'ear me, gal? Says he'll pay extra to be bound in leather with a gold tool!*

'Owzat for kinks?'

Bernard closed his eyes and shuddered . . .

He opened them again and gave a start. Had he heard aright? Was the girl Janice calling him from the bedroom?

'Are you there?'

She was!

Bernard leapt from the sofa, staggered and nearly fell; shrugged into his silk dressing-gown; fumbled for his slippers, could not find them and decided to go barefoot. His hand trembled as he opened the bedroom door and looked inside.

'Did you call?' he asked.

'It's this bedside-lamp. I think the light bulb's gone. Do you have a spare, please?'

She was sitting up in bed with a book propped up against her knees. Her crisp, flaxen curls were spread out across the pillow – his pillow – and the end of the bed-sheet – his best, Regency candy-striped bedsheet – suavely described the curve of her unbelievably slender waist. Between these two limits, she was exiguously clad in what Bernard's limited knowledge of feminine apparel led him to suppose was a 'shirtwaist' or a 'slip'.

'I – I don't have a spare,' he said, fixing his gaze upon the crown of her head. 'But I'll swap it for the bulb up there.' Pointing to the light in the middle of the ceiling.

'I wouldn't put you to all that trouble,' she said.

'It's no trouble, I assure you,' said Bernard, ponderously reaching for a chair.

'It's a long way up there,' she persisted. 'And suddenly I don't feel like reading any more.' The bed gave a creak as she laid the book aside and settled down.

Bernard placed the chair exactly under the light

fitting; narrowing his eyes to get the alignment right.

'You don' – you don' think I'm capable of getting up there,' he said aggressively.

'You're so wrong,' said Janice sweetly. 'I think you're tremendously capable, Mr Davis.'

'Well, I am,' declared Bernard. 'An' – an' after I have done this, I'll walk a chalked line, or any other feat you call upon me to perform.'

'And such a terrible bully, too!' was her cheerful comment.

Bernard gathered up one leg and placed the foot carefully upon the chair. He used the support of the chair-back to bring the rest of himself up. The light bulb was just within the reach of his extended hand. He touched it; let out a yelp of pain when it burnt his fingers; scowled when he thought he heard a muffled laugh from the direction of the bed.

He fished in his dressing-gown pocket, and leered triumphantly when he brought out a handkerchief.

'Watch this,' he said, 'as with one clean movement, I reach up . . . reach up and . . .'

She cried out in alarm, as the chair's wild oscillations increased to pendulum proportions, with Bernard still stolidly reaching up, and was out of bed and half-way to the rescue when man and chair overturned in one piece, to measure their respective lengths across the room. Bernard fell short of the room's shortest dimension by a foot, so that the back of his head connected with the wainscoting.

He knew no more.

At the end of the long night, he opened his eyes and saw street lights coming at him through the cracks between the curtains, and heard the roar of wind pounding the outside walls and window frames. The sound started a trip-hammer going in his brain, so that he was forced to shut his eyes and cry out with pain.

When he opened them again, the room light was on, and a young woman was standing by his bedside with a cup and saucer on a tray. She was curiously attired in a man's dressing-gown turned up at the cuffs. The thing had no buttons; with clinical detachment, he saw enough to judge that she was probably nude underneath it.

'Who are you?' he asked her.

'Oh!' she exclaimed gravely. And again: 'Oh! I rather feared that might have happened.'

She laid the tray on the bedside-table and sat down on the edge of his bed, taking up the cup and saucer.

'*What's* happened?' he asked.

'You've got concussion,' she said. 'I looked it up in the encyclopaedia, which was quite informative but rather alarming as to details. Drink this – it's a cup of hot, sweet tea. It wasn't specifically recommended in the encyclopaedia, but I seem to remember it's a sovereign remedy for shock. Do you feel any shock?'

'I don't feel anything in particular,' he said. 'Only a splitting headache, and a sensation of being very far away from everything.'

She put the cup to his lips and he sipped the syrupy brew.

'It says in the book,' she told him, 'that concussion in its mildest form leaves the patient unconscious for a brief while.'

'How long . . . how long have I been unconscious?'

'Nearly twenty-four hours,' she said. 'But you also had a night's sleep to make up, and you were as drunk as a lord at the time.'

'Twenty-four hours? But . . .'

'It mentioned the headache,' she said. 'And you can expect that to last long after the other symptoms have cleared up, within about forty-eight hours. There is also some impairment of mental function, it says. And there could be a loss of memory for events before the injury or for a period after it.' She looked at him with her head on one side, and a wayward twist of flaxen curl caressed her tanned and freckled cheek. 'How's your memory?'

He took a deep breath, and said: 'Who are you?'

'Forget me,' she said. 'Do you know who *you* are?'

'Yes,' he said. 'I'm inside myself, so I know all about myself. Only . . . I just don't seem to be able to lay my hands on exactly who I am at the moment. It's just round the corner, but it will come back.'

'Finish your tea,' she said. 'Then we can all get some sleep. I expect you'll have all the answers by morning. I hope so, at any rate, because we've got a big day — starting with the arrival of the mail.'

She stood up, and began to untie the sash of the dressing-gown. He watched her with the mildly pleasant sense of detachment that she had aroused in him from the first.

'Please don't be offended,' he said. 'But do we happen to be married . . . or anything?'

'Another thing it mentioned in the book,' she said, 'was that some patients become uninhibited and talkative. Do you feel uninhibited and talkative?'

'What do I usually call you?' he persisted.

'You do chatter on,' she said. The dressing-gown fell in a silken pool at her feet. Her body was deeply tanned all over, and as she turned to switch out the centre light, she showed a mole in the small of her deeply-cleft back.

When she slid between the sheets beside him, she said: 'How's your memory now?'

'Not very good,' he told her.

She said: 'On a blank sheet of paper, free of any mark, the freshest and most beautiful characters can be written.'

CHAPTER IX

Bernard's first thought in the pre-dawn light was: why had his brother Alec not called round to see him? Alec must have tried to reach him by telephone, following the breakdown of their rendezvous on Saturday night. Had he attempted to visit the flat, only to get himself waylaid and kidnapped by the watching Bolsheviks? Was he, even now, lying in torment in the cottage on the Doncaster road of which the girl Janice had spoken so calmly?

He leapt out of bed, wincing when a stab of pain jolted from temple to temple, threw on his dressing-gown and went to look for Janice. She was in the kitchen, fully dressed in après-ski pants and sweater. She looked round briefly from the frying-pan when he came in.

'Hello,' she said. 'How's it all feeling?'

He sat down weakly on a stool by the fridge. 'The last thing I remember with any clarity,' he said, 'was a stupid argument with you, over supper, about the nature of art. What happened after that?'

'A lot of things,' she said. 'Fried egg?'

'No, thank you.'

'You concussed yourself trying to get a light bulb down from the ceiling,' she said. 'And you've been out – with intervals of being comparatively in – ever since. And now it's Monday morning.'

'Monday?' he cried. 'Good lord, it never is!'

'How's the head?'

'Terrible,' he said. 'I wouldn't have believed that anyone could suffer such pain and live, or stay sane.'

'No other symptoms? Memory all right?'

'Except that the whole thing – everything that happened after that argument at supper – is a total blank. What did you say?'

'Nothing,' she murmured. 'Coffee?'

'Yes, please.'

Sipping gratefully, he told her of his concern about his elder brother. Her reply was casual, even indifferent.

'They could have taken him,' she said. 'But there would hardly be any point at this stage. Grabbing hold of everyone in sight is the sort of tactical inelegance that professionals don't succumb to – and, believe me, those people are professionals. You're their prime target. And, anyhow, they don't have the manpower available to act quite so broadly. Is the postman ever seriously late?'

'Never,' said Bernard. 'Ten minutes to seven every morning, right on the button.'

The kitchen clock in the shape of a frying-pan said it was a quarter to seven. Bernard felt a prickle of eerie anticipation, for was he not about to receive a visitation that could with some truth be described as being from beyond the grave?

Janice scooped up her fried egg and laid it between two pieces of toast.

'With my proclivities,' she said, 'I can't afford this kind

of calorie intake. I'm only hoping that today's mental and physical demands will provide the bonus of radically speeding up my rate of metabolism.'

'You don't need to bother about your figure,' said Bernard. 'It looks just about right to me.'

'Thank you,' she said. 'I thought you'd never notice.'

At that moment, they both clearly heard the unmistakable click of a letterbox, followed by the muffled thud of something landing on the carpet at the foot of the stairs.

'I forgot to mention,' said Bernard, 'that he's sometimes a few minutes early.'

They ran out of the kitchen. Unbolting and unlocking the upper door, they looked down the staircase. There was a neat bundle of envelopes fastened together with an elastic band. He made to go down, but she stayed his arm.

'Go to the window,' she said. 'Check if it's the usual postman.'

He nodded. A few moments later, looking out, he saw a familiar figure crossing the road. The man was hatless as usual, and the gale must have died down, because the fringe of hair round his bald patch was scarcely disturbed: he saw it quite clearly in the street lights. And there was no sign of the watcher opposite.

He turned and nodded to Janice. 'It's him.'

Descending the stairs to pick up the mail, he felt like a tomb robber going down into a vault: the whole thing seemed so significant: sacramental. The top envelope was his football pool coupon. Then a couple of circulars. Then – and he felt a distinct *frisson* – a foolscap envelope of thick legalistic bond, with a typed address, and the name of the solicitors embossed on the flap.

'Is it there?' she called down.

He held it up.

She had the sense of occasion to pour them both fresh coffee in clean cups; and she sat without a word of interruption as he read to himself the strange testament of his departed sire.

'Well, Bernard,' (*written in Father's spiky, continental-looking handwriting: the letter was enclosed in another envelope within the solicitor's envelope*) . . .
'By the time you receive this, I shall have gone my way. And good riddance, I can hear you all cry. To hell with the old devil! I know. I've always known what you think of the old man. Damn this arm. It's nearly useless. I shall have to rest it . . .'
(*The letter broke off, and was resumed further down the page in a more ordered handwriting, as if on a later occasion, when the old man's arm – half-paralysed after his stroke – had been in better shape. It went straight into narrative form, without any preamble.*)
'March of 1919 found me a volunteer in the Tenth Workers' Battalion, called the Dnieper battalion. Marching on Kiev. Before that, three years as the Tsar's conscript on the East Prussian front. Fighting the Germans. A starving farm-boy with a rifle. Then desertion. They hunted us like dogs, the Tsar's military police. The Bolsheviks gave us soup, so we became Bolsheviks.

'After we had taken Kiev – the looting. From the Cathedral, they took the mummies of saints and archbishops and burnt them in the square. I came upon this drunken comrade holding the famous Gregory reliquary that he had taken from the chapel nearby. Thinking I was going to steal it off him, he took his pistol to me. But I was quicker with my bayonet.

'I became a deserter for the second time. Fled northwards. Near Nogilev, I came upon this one-armed Guards' officer and his chauffeur in the broken-down automobile. The pig called upon me to change his wheel. Ordered me. I shot them both.

'They had taught me to drive in the Tsar's army. I took the automobile. And his white Guards' uniform. And his identity. He was the *boyar* Prince Davydov. It was all in his papers. In the back of his automobile was even Tokay and boxes of sugared almonds. I drove on northwards. With me was the bauble from the chapel at Kiev – the famous reliquary, all diamonds, rubies and pearls. The rest you know . . .'

(*The narrative closed here. The letter was resumed on a separate sheet, and in a crabbed and disorganized hand that spoke of painful effort in its execution.*)

'Bernard, I have not had a good life. I damn you all as wastrels, my sons. I go to my grave unloved, unwanted. Once I would have left you the reliquary, but I have changed my mind. Make your own ways in the world – as I did. I have done enough for you.

'I brought the bauble out of Holy Russia, and when I go it will go also. For ever! James is a fool, but he has had his orders and will carry them out. By the time you have read this, James will have disposed of the Gregory reliquary – he has had four days, more than enough time.'

(*The letter ended as abruptly as it had begun, and without any signature.*)

Bernard, perched on the kitchen stool with his head splitting with pain, stared down for a long time at his father's testament, trying to absorb its stark phraseology that sounded so alien to the coarse vernacular of the old man.

Presently, Janice said: 'What does it tell us?'

'The treasure's disappeared for ever,' he said. 'I obviously wasn't alone in Father's confidence. That was always my assumption, and entirely unfounded. James has disposed of it.' He passed her the last page of the letter, putting the other page in his pocket. 'The rest of it's all private, family stuff,' he explained. There didn't seem any reason why a stranger should know the truth about the spurious Davydovs. Leave that for the Davises.

While she was reading, he went into the bedroom and took down the encyclopaedia at Volume E–G. He quickly found what he was seeking.

GREGORY THE LESSER, SAINT (c.1217–1238), a Russian martyr put to death at Novgorod. The particulars of his martyrdom are obscure, but according to tradition he remained to defy the Mongol invasion of 1237–40, was ordered to be tortured, and died in consequence. His iconography reflects the circumstances of his death: total castration. In c.1350, his remains were moved to St Sophia Cathedral, Kiev. The following year, he was first named in the canon of the Orthodox Eastern Church. In c.1440 there was caused to be built a chapel to his memory adjacent to the cathedral, in which reposed a Reliquary containing the alleged severed member of the saint. This Reliquary, richly inset with diamonds, rubies and pearls (the diamonds and pearls symbolizing his purity, the rubies his martyrdom), was widely revered by the peasant women of the Ukraine, up until the Revolution (q.v.), as a sovereign remedy against conception. Its contraceptive powers were unfortunately never put to scientific test, since the Reliquary and its contents disappeared during the destruction of the chapel when the Bolshevik forces occupied the city in March, 1919.

See R. Standish (ed.) *Grant's Lives of the Orthodox Eastern Church's Saints*, vol. ii, pp. 133–136 (1899).

Janice walked swiftly into the bedroom, the page of the letter in her hand.

'How has your brother destroyed this thing?' she demanded. 'And what was this Gregory reliquary he writes about?'

Bernard handed her the volume and tapped the page at the relevant entry. While she was reading it, he looked around the room, seeking for inspiration; more precisely, for a spark that would ignite a powder train that led to an idea that was forming, all unbidden, in some dusty corner of his mind. There was something in the bedroom: something that associated with his brother James and James's special capacity as a disposal agent. What was it?

He saw his answer . . .

'No wonder the Soviets want to get their hands on this thing!' exclaimed Janice.

Bernard cried: 'That's it! That's how James dumped the reliquary! And we'll never get it back now – any of us!'

He pointed to a calendar that hung over his dressing-table. It had come from James and his family the previous Christmas, and showed an idealized scene of a motor-cruiser planing grandly through Mediterranean blue seas, with a family of handsome, happy, top-grade advertising material aboard.

'James took it out in his motor-boat! He must have received Father's instructions on Friday. His boat's at a marina on the south bank of the Humber. He took the reliquary out of the estuary, out into the North Sea — and dumped it overboard!'

Janice thought for a moment.

'Not in the weather we've been having since Friday!' she snapped. 'Not in a whole gale! He'd need a lifeboat and a lifeboat's crew to get out beyond Spurn Head!'

'You're right! By Jove, you're right!' cried Bernard.

Both their gazes sped towards the window; to the dawn light breaking behind the still clouds massed over the estuary.

'But – *this* morning . . .' she began.

'He'd have a chance now! Come on!'

'Where does he live, your brother?'

'Only just round the corner from Father's house, in Cliff Gardens,' said Bernard. 'How do we get there – on foot?'

'Safer by my car,' she said, pulling on her leather coat. 'And we may need it to go on farther.'

'If the car's still there!' he said glumly.

'Our people will have been keeping a round-the-clock guard on it,' she replied. 'This isn't Moscow, you know.'

Down the stairs and out into the street and the first of the wintry daylight. The wind had almost entirely gone and there was a haze of warmish rain in the air, as if it had been sprayed at them from an atomizer. They ran all the way to the back street, and her yellow Fiat was still there, under the lamp by the Chinese Take-Away. At that hour, the Orientals were already at work behind their steamy window.

'You made the remark,' said Bernard, as they drove off, 'to the effect that you didn't wonder that the Bolsheviks wanted to get their hands on the reliquary. How's this?'

'It's the sort of thing they hate most of all,' replied the girl. 'Stalin's taunt about how many divisions did the Pope have? – that was just whistling in the dark. They're really scared of religion. I mean religion at the way-out level particularly; the lunatic fringe level; the level of the superstitious peasantry. I don't have the background on the Gregory reliquary at my fingertips (I can soon get it), but from all the muscle the Soviets have disposed, it's obviously in the big league of saintly relics. The sort that draws mass-pilgrimages, mass-hysteria, and all that stuff. Which way now?'

'Straight across the main street and second right,' said Bernard, pointing. 'But tell me – why do *you* want it? I mean, why does Her Majesty's Government want the Gregory reliquary?'

'This business,' she said, 'this business I'm in, it's got so snarled up that we've not only forgotten the rules, but we also often lose sight of our immediate goals. So we proceed pragmatically. The simple answer to your question is: we want the reliquary because the Soviets want it; and the more they want it, the harder we'll try to stop them. Is this the turning?'

'Yes,' said Bernard. 'That's James's place, the one with the garage doors open. Oh, God – that means we may be too late!'

The light came on behind the front door of the house

before Bernard and the girl had got out of the car, and his sister-in-law was standing on the threshold in her nightdress and robe before they were half-way down the path.

'Oh, Bernard!' she cried. 'Am I glad to see you. I've been trying to phone you all weekend.'

'The phone's been out of order,' said Bernard. 'Janice, this is Maureen Davis, my sister-in-law. Maureen, this is Janice um . . .'

The two females nodded to each other cautiously. Maureen had been crying. She shut the door, but made no move to ask them into the sitting-room.

'On top of everything else,' she cried, 'have you heard about Kitty?'

'You mean Ekaterina,' said Bernard with a touch of malice. 'I hear she's decided to call herself Princess Ekaterina.'

'She went missing last evening,' cried Maureen.

'Oh!' Bernard and Janice exchanged glances.

'She'd been acting strangely ever since Father passed away,' said Maureen. 'But even before Alec had time to report her missing to the police, he had this phone call from the cinema. She was there.'

'Well, that was all right, then,' said Bernard. 'What we've really come about, Maureen, is . . .'

'No, it isn't all right!' cried his sister-in-law. 'They were showing a double-feature sex film programme!'

'Well,' said Bernard reasonably. 'She's over eighteen.'

'She was sitting in the back row with a silver-gilt coronet on her head!' wailed Maureen.

'It's eccentric,' conceded Bernard. 'But not illegal.'

'Naked!'

'*Wha-a-at?*'

'Naked as the day she was born! She'd taken off her coat and was just sitting there. In a coronet. Eating an ice-cream. It was awful. Alec's managed to get her into a private nursing home, but . . .'

'No wonder he never had time to look in at the flat,' said Bernard to Janice, and she nodded.

'I would have come to see you,' said Maureen. She had started to cry again. 'But James has been so strange and jumpy. Ever since that letter was delivered by hand from the solicitors.'

'When was that?' cried Bernard.

'Fu-Friday afternoon,' sobbed his sister-in-law. 'And ever since then, he's been like a cat on hot bricks. Ringing for a weather report. Tapping the barometer. Drinking a lot. I've been worried out of my mind about him, Bernard, I really have.'

'Where is your husband now, Mrs Davis?' demanded Janice briskly.

'He was up by five,' wailed Maureen. 'And he went out half an hour ago. He – he didn't even come into my room and kiss me good morning.'

'So – you don't know what he was wearing?' asked Bernard.

'No. Except that I heard his gumboots when he opened the garage doors,' said Maureen. 'And I've just noticed that he's taken his oilskins.'

Bernard and the girl were half-way to the marina before the dawn sun had made any headway through the clouds. It was still raining, but there was hardly any wind – an unstable situation that, considering the then prevailing weather, was scarcely likely to last.

Grey water, and a line of smudgy brown that described

the north bank of the river two miles away through the misty rain, which was now so fine that it barely marked the oily surface of the water. Away to the right, the distant buildings, towers, steeples and chimneys of Hull, rising from the greyness, fading into the background like cut-out cardboard flats.

There was no sign of life at the marina; those boats that were in the water were clustered at their jetties and pontoons, masts gently swaying.

'Which is his boat?' demanded Janice.

'It's a motor-cruiser,' said Bernard. 'About thirty feet long and painted white. I scarcely know it. Only seen it a couple of times, and never been out in it.'

'They all look like that here, apart from the sailing boats,' snapped Janice.

'He might have already left,' said Bernard. They had come upon James's funereal black saloon in the marina car park. 'But I can't see anything out there in the tideway.'

At that moment there came to their ears, across the still water, the muffled sound of a diesel engine coughing itself reluctantly into life.

'There it is!' cried Bernard.

At the far side of the marina, a cloud of steam and exhaust smoke was drifting back from the stern of a small cruiser. They were half-way to it when a figure in yellow oilskins came out of a companionway and looked about him.

'JAMES!' roared Bernard.

The other swung round and presented a startled face to them, one hand reaching to unfasten one of the lines that held the boat to the pontoon. James was wearing his yachting cap. He being of the same breed as the actor who blacked himself all over to play Othello, Bernard made the shrewd guess that his brother would be clad in boating attire from the skin outwards, for the enterprise.

'What are you doing here?' demanded James, as they stepped on to his deck.

'Put a knot in that rope and let's go below,' said Bernard, and James sourly obeyed.

The little cabin below the wheelhouse smelt of tarred rope, lavatory cleanser and stale food scraps. Janice bumped her head on a beam and swore quietly. James joined them, eyeing the girl in a truculent manner.

'Make it snappy, whatever it is,' said the amateur seaman. 'I've got tides to watch.'

There did not seem any point, at that stage, in beating about the bush. 'You won't be going out today, James,' said Bernard. 'No matter what your orders from Father, that thing isn't to be disposed of.'

'What do . . . what do *you* know about it?' James was inclined to a high blood pressure; right now, his face was red as raw beef, and his lower lip stuck out. 'And who's *she*, might I ask?' he added rudely, indicating the girl.

'More of that later, James,' said Bernard patiently. 'Hand the thing over, there's a good chap, then we'll all sit down and talk about it.'

'I'm damned if I will!' cried his brother.

The Biretta was in Janice's hand when she took it out of her pocket; she pointed it straight at James's middle.

'Produce it!' she said coldly. 'Now!'

'Oh, how bloody ridiculous!' James turned to his brother, blustering. 'Tell your lady-friend to put away her imitation gun before I chuck the pair of you ashore, neck and crop!'

'It isn't an imitation gun, James,' said Bernard.

'Oh, come on, man! What do you take me for?'

'Watch!' murmured Janice, and she aimed the pistol across the cabin. The report was deafening in the narrow confines of the boat. The bullet smashed its way through a cupboard door over the bunk, and there was a tinkle of broken glass from beyond. The spent cartridge-case hit the deck and rolled into a corner.

'Good God!' faltered James, and his heavy face slowly drained of all colour.

'Get it, there's a good chap,' said Bernard gently, as Janice put away the gun.

On the stern of James's boat, just forward of the transom, a rectangle of decking lifted on the removal of half a dozen screws. Inside, neatly set above the propeller shaft, was a secret compartment measuring about four feet by two feet by two feet. Nestling down there in this miniature hold was a small metal-bound wooden chest with the type of lid known in the antique trade as a melon top. James reached and lifted the chest with an ease that suggested it was quite light, and carried it back into the cabin, where he laid it on the table.

'I don't have the key,' he said defiantly to Bernard, with an uneasy sidelong glance at the girl. 'Father always kept the key. I've never seen it open.' There was a stout padlock joining two hasps that held the lid shut.

'You've got tools in this boat,' said Janice implacably, hand in gun pocket. 'Force it open.'

The end of a marlinespike rammed between the hasps prised them out of the old wood like rotten teeth, and Bernard lifted back the lid.

'There it is – the Gregory reliquary!'

It was shaped something like a child's Noah's Ark, of

worm-eaten wood and gold filigree. And the filigree was smothered in diamonds, rubies and pearls – though about a quarter of the settings were empty and eyeless. In the centre, and surrounded by rubies of the largest size, was a window of smoky bottle glass, through which could dimly be discerned the relic within: a fragment of blackened twig held in place by two loops of gold wire – the minuscule member of Gregory the Lesser, patron saint of contraception.

'Great Scott!' breathed James in awe.

'I think I'll go and phone my people and tell them to come and fetch it under suitable guard,' said Janice.

'There's a public phone box near the entrance to the car park,' said Bernard.

She was back in five minutes, and found the brothers deep in conversation, to which she listened, while she put the reliquary back into its chest and secured the lid with a length of cord.

'Every New Year's Day,' said James, 'for the last ten years, I've had to bring the chest to Father, who took it into his study and came out with it about half an hour later. I've had charge of it for the last ten years, but have never had the slightest inkling of what was in it.'

'You were the guardian,' said Bernard, 'and I the messenger boy. Every New Year's Day, Father prised out the gems he would be requiring me to sell in the following twelve months. You were due to bring it to him again at the end of December; the diamond I sold in London on Friday must have been the last of the nineteen seventy-four batch.'

'I got scared when I had this letter by hand from the solicitors on Friday,' said James. 'In it was Father's order for me to put to sea immediately and dump the chest in deep water. Naturally, with a full gale blowing, it was quite out of the question.'

'Father was all landsman,' said Bernard. 'I don't suppose it ever occurred to him that the weather could provide a snag to his plans. And then you rang me on Saturday morning.'

'By then I was really worried,' said James. 'If anything, the weather was worse. In his letter, Father hinted at the most dire penalties that would follow if I disobeyed him in any detail. Frankly, Bernard, I was scared he'd made provision to cut me out of his will if I failed him. It was then I had half a notion to confide in you, since I could hardly confide in Alec without his telling his damned wife. I suppose you've heard all about her?'

'Yes,' said Bernard. 'Poor old Alec. As if he doesn't have enough worries on his plate.' He looked at Janice, who was knotting the cord about the melon-topped chest. 'How long are your people going to be?' he asked her.

'They'll be here any minute,' said Janice.

In fact, they were already entering the marina. Bernard was the first to see them through the cabin porthole: a smallish black van approaching through the car park and out on to the jetty. James went half-way up the companionway and waved. The driver of the van pulsed his headlights in response, and turned to come towards them.

It was not till the van was nearly abreast that Bernard was able to see the manner of men it contained; when the four of them got out and started to walk along the pontoons, he realized what big, dangerous-looking characters they were. After all, he had only seen them in head and shoulders before – and that behind a steamed-up window.

And now that the van was broadside on, he was able to read the legend on the side:

> *Cathay Flower Take-Away and Deliver*
> *Finest Chinese Cuisine*
> *Scunthorpe*

Something prodded the small of his back.

'Just put your hands on your head, darling,' said Janice. 'We don't want to end a beautiful acquaintance with a lot of messiness, do we?'

CHAPTER X

The Chinese were perhaps fifty yards away, and ambling in no particular hurry along the pontoons towards them, when Bernard called sharply to his brother, who was still standing on the companionway.

'Cast off the lines, James! Shove off – and let the tide take us out of here!'

Simultaneously, he turned to face the girl, meeting the expression on her face, which changed from smiling triumph to anger, and then to ice-cold murder. She grimaced as she dug the muzzle of the Biretta into his chest and pulled the trigger. There was a click – and her face crumpled like that of a thwarted child.

She let him take the pistol from her.

'I'm not very politically orientated,' he said. 'But I do happen to know the jargon you people trot out about art. The stuff you gave me over supper on Saturday was right out of the Chairman's little red book. It didn't worry me greatly at the time, but, just as a precaution, I took the six cartridges from the magazine leaving you only the one up the spout.'

From his pocket, he took the handful of nickel-jacketed jujubes and snicked them into the butt of the pistol.

'Damn you!' she said – far from the pride of the School First XI Hockey grown to triumphant British womanhood now.

'I dare say,' he smiled at her. 'How's it going, James?'

'All gone!' cried James. 'We're away!'

The irresistible fingers of the Humber's tide bore the freed cruiser swiftly away from its pontoon. Seeing this, the four Chinese broke into a run. They reached the water's edge and stood there, puzzled and irresolute. Bernard waved to them through the cabin porthole.

'Call out to them, James,' he said, 'that there's been a change of plan.'

James cupped his hands round his mouth and repeated the message to the men on the pontoon. It won him four broad grins and an acknowledging wave.

'Good,' said Bernard. 'We don't want to be pursued by a hail of flying lead.'

'I'll start the engine,' said James. He glanced doubtfully at the girl, who was now sitting on the bunk, face expressionless. 'I take it your lady-friend is no longer – er – one of us?'

'That's right,' said Bernard. 'Anywhere we can lock her up safely for the time being?'

'There's the forepeak,' James suggested. 'It's got everything there, including fresh water and a loo.'

Janice looked up and met Bernard's gaze.

'Just how did *you* people get involved in this?' he asked.

'It wasn't difficult,' she said. 'Garbisian and Waller practically hung neon signs on you. Our boys could scarcely miss that something was going on.'

'Your boys in Scunthorpe . . . the Chinese Take-Away thing . . . how long has *that* been going on?'

Her blue eyes were very wide and surprised. 'Since for ever,' she said. 'What else would they do with their spare time?'

'Good lord,' said Bernard, taking her arm. Unresisting, she let him guide her into the narrow compartment in the front end of the boat. She did not look round as he closed the door.

It was twenty miles down the rivers – down Humber and Trent – to a jetty near Althorpe bridge, where they tied up the boat and left it. Bernard had knocked on the door of the forepeak and called out to the girl that she would have to make what shift she could with her imprisonment for a while – but he had received no acknowledgement.

They thumbed a lift into Scunthorpe from a passing truck. During the river journey, Bernard had thoroughly briefed his brother about those elements of the situation to which he wanted James to apply himself. James was carrying the chest; when they parted company at the junction of Doncaster Road and the High Street, he knew the role he had to play.

'Lock up the reliquary,' reiterated Bernard, 'then deal with Garbisian. We're stuck with his body again, and we've got to find a way to dispose of it. If the Aston's been towed away or broken into, try and give me a ring immediately, and if my phone's still off, come to me. If all's well, get the spare tyre from under the rear end, put it on, and drive straight to the mortuary.'

'And I'll get in touch with you when the body's safely under lock and key,' said James, who was quite enjoying the situation. 'See you, Bernard.'

'Good luck, James,' said his brother.

It was one-thirty when Bernard let himself into the flat, and Monica's was still closed for lunch, a meal which – as he knew – she mostly ate in a café some distance down the street. He scarcely had time to take off his coat before the telephone rang.

It couldn't be James already. Nor was it.

'Mr Davis, we see that you have returned home. You are very lucky still to be alive.'

'Who's this?' demanded Bernard.

'Well-wishers, Mr Davis,' came the smooth reply. 'And may we convey our sincere condolences for the death of the *boyar*, the former Excellency Prince Davydov. In the apt words of that great dean of St Paul's: "Never send to know for whom the bell tolls," etcetera. Do we make ourselves clear?'

The Bolsheviks. They had been watching for him to come in, and now they had restored his telephone. What next?

'What can I do for you?' asked Bernard.

'We believe, Mr Davis – but here we may be entirely mistaken – that you are in possession of a certain object.'

'I have it!' said Bernard bluntly. 'The Gregory reliquary! Do you want to make a deal?'

This drew forth from his caller a sharp intake of breath and a moment's awed silence. And then: 'Well, it is clear that we all know what we are talking about, Mr Davis. Er . . .'

'Do you want it?' snapped Bernard. 'Or don't you? If you don't, there's plenty who do.'

'You proceed hastily, Mr Davis,' came the reply. 'There would be certain conditions to be met. Certain assurances . . .'

'You bet your sweet life there would be,' said Bernard brusquely. 'You don't get your hands on that reliquary till I have your assurances that my family and I will be more than adequately rewarded, and guaranteed one hundred per cent freedom from reprisals. You come up with a deal along those lines and we'll talk further. Good day to you.'

'Mr Davis . . .'

'Get on to the Kremlin,' said Bernard. 'Get them to agree a really attractive proposition, and you've probably got yourself a deal. Good day.'

He poured himself a drink, noting with some pride that his hand was quite steady. It took him ten minutes to sink the three fingers of scotch: ten minutes of hard thinking. At the end of it he picked up the phone and dialled a Scunthorpe number.

'Cathay Flower Take-Away at your service. Orders delivered within the hour, or ready for collection in ten minutes. We live only to serve you. Was there anything, please?'

'This is Bernard Davis,' said Bernard. 'I'm speaking for Janice. Miss Janice, you know.'

'Ah, Mr Davis. Is Miss Janice there, please? We are very puzzled . . .'

'Everything's changed,' said Bernard. 'She told me to give you these instructions. Listen carefully.'

'Yes, Mr Davis. I have a pencil and paper poised. A moment, please. The other telephone is ringing . . . Cathay Flower Take-Away at your service. Orders delivered within the hour . . .'

Bernard placed the receiver on the table and went over to pour himself another drink. A minute later, he returned and picked up the phone again.

'... and two portions of the egg foo yung. Beef Cathay with oyster sauce I can strongly recommend, madam. Yes, it will be ready when you call at seven o'clock. At your service, madam. We live only to serve you ...

'Mr Davis, my apologies. Please continue.'

'The thing that has to be collected,' said Bernard. 'Did Miss Janice give you any details about it?'

'No, Mr Davis,' came the reply. 'Miss Janice merely informed us that the item was to be collected and passed on.'

'Right. Well, here's the new arrangement: Miss Janice says you're to pick it up at the rear entrance to Fitch, Davis and Sons, undertakers, at nine-fifteen tomorrow morning. Just drive your van into the yard and it'll be there waiting for you. Got that?'

'Nine-fifteen. We shall be there, tell Miss Janice. Is that all, Mr Davis?'

'Just be on time, or there may be incalculable complications.'

'Cathay Flower Take-Away is always on time, Mr Davis. We live only to serve you. He, he!'

At six-thirty p.m. Moscow time, Glinka reported himself to the Rokossovsky Prospect in answer to an urgent summons from the Controller. He found her alone.

As ever, she kept him waiting and dying by inches while she finished what she was about; five minutes passed before she laid aside the file on which she was working; lit a fresh cigarette from the butt of the other.

'The reliquary has been located,' she said. 'Bernard Davis has it in his possession, or claims he has. Declares himself ready to trade with us. Further complications:

he states that – quote – if we don't want it, there's plenty who do. Your observations on that, Glinka.'

Glinka clasped his bony hands together, tugging at the knobbly finger joints till they cracked like dry twigs underfoot. His bearded face looked upwards, as if seeking inspiration from the baroque plaster-work of the ceiling.

Presently, he said: 'Comrade Controller, all the evidence suggests that the Americans have been entirely deceived by their fraudulent agents. It is likely that they are still not even aware of the reliquary's existence; that, at least, is the conclusion of the four sufferers from acute anxiety neurosis whom I have put on to examining all negative aspects of the situation. No worry from the Americans, then.'

'The Chinese?' grated the Controller.

'The Chinese – ah!' Glinka cracked his finger joints anew. 'Some cause for anxiety there, Comrade Controller. As we know, their female agent has been closeted with Bernard Davis since Saturday night.'

'Since *your* people let him slip through their fingers, Glinka!'

Glinka swallowed hard. 'I submit, Comrade Controller, that it has not worked to our disadvantage: even after long negotiations with the agent of the Chinese, Bernard Davis is still willing to do a deal with us.'

'That deal must be concluded, Glinka,' said the woman. 'At all costs. We cannot accept the risk of the reliquary falling into Chinese hands. With it, they could cause incalulable dissension within and without the borders of the Soviet Union.' She tapped the file before her. 'I have a scenario that projects what would happen if they set up a shrine for the Gregory relic just over the border from Kazakh Socialist Soviet Republic: it postulates mass migrations of superstitious peasantry within twenty years; fifty per cent fall of birth-rate through mass auto-suggestion within thirty.'

'It must not happen, Comrade Controller!' cried Glinka fervently. 'It must not!'

The woman held up a doughy white hand. 'It will not, Glinka,' she intoned. 'It will not! We will trade with Bernard Davis, either for the reliquary or for a guarantee of its total destruction under the supervision of your people in Scunthorpe. Bernard Davis, in his turn, demands adequate reward and freedom from reprisals for his family and himself. This is the difficulty: to contrive a sufficiently attractive reward and a convincing and totally watertight assurance of perpetual inviolability for the Davis family.'

'An assurance that we could not repudiate as soon as the reliquary is in our possession?' asked Glinka wistfully.

'An assurance guaranteed by circumstances that would manifestly make it impossible for us to repudiate,' replied the Controller. 'And I am open to suggestions, Glinka.'

'I will work on it right away, Comrade,' said Glinka. And when she reached for the file again, he turned to leave. He paused at the door. 'By the way, Comrade Controller,' he asked, 'has Major Kornilov managed to get at the truth concerning the death of Garbisian?'

'The agents in question still persist that they did not deliberately kill Garbisian,' replied the woman. 'This is obviously incorrect. Major Kornilov has been . . . removed . . . from the enquiry.'

Glinka shuddered. 'I see,' he whispered.

'One thing more, Comrade Glinka.'

'Yes, Comrade Controller?'

'You say that you are unmarried?'

'That – that is so, Comrade Controller.'

'Then I wonder – ' the rare smile marginally softened the expression in her dull blue eyes – 'I wonder if you would care to have supper with me tonight – after we have concluded the arrangements for the deal with Bernard Davis?'

It was at nine a.m. that an angry phone call from the Secretary of State galvanized Steiner hastily to assemble an *ad hoc* committee to discuss the newest developments on the Davydov Situation.

Williams was still shaving, but he said he would be right over – and, no, he did not think it would be necessary, or even advisable, to bring his aide Tom Jackson; goddamnit, hadn't Jackson done enough harm already?

At that short notice, it was not easy to make up a meaningful quorum, so Steiner was reduced to trying for the former head of Tsarist Russia (Residuals); but Dade, when reached at his new retirement home in Florida, flatly refused to be brought up to Washington by Air Force supersonic fighter. DeSoto simply was not available to his friends.

Padding out, then, with fairly low-grade people from the agencies, Steiner finally collected a quorum of eight, and they met in the sixth-floor conference-room just as the chimes of the half ten were dying in the east wind.

Steiner began: 'Gentlemen, I had a call from the Secretary of State and he burnt my tail about this, I want you to know he put it hard to me that maybe someone had bungled on this situation. Now, let me have your reactions to this.'

'Mr Chairman,' said Williams, 'I want to be the first to say that in some regards we over-reacted to this situation, and that in other regards we under-reacted. And when I say 'us', I mean *some* of us.'

'Specifically – Tom Jackson over-reacted?' prompted Steiner.

'Right, Mr Chairman!' confirmed Williams. 'I want to be the first to say that, in many respects, Tom did a great job with the Davydov Situation. But I'm here to say that the proposal – his proposal – to move the Sixth Fleet to Gibraltar was a blunder.'

'In view of the fact,' supplied Steiner, 'that, according to Naval Intelligence, the Soviets have moved fleet units, in obvious retaliation, to the very estuary of the River Humber, to Humberside itself.'

'Damn right, Mr Chairman!' said Williams. 'And I'm not surprised you caught holy hell from the Secretary of State on account of this. And the last thing Mr Secretary will want to see now is anything that suggests a snow job on the part of this *ad hoc* committee.'

The chairman shuddered, and passed his handkerchief over his bald head.

'Anything you can suggest, Joe,' he pleaded. 'Anything that would be of aid in this situation . . .'

'Referring back to my opening remark,' said Williams, 'that in some regards we under-reacted. For this I take my fair share of responsibility. Clearly, it would have been of aid to have given more support to our agent Waller in Scunthorpe. As we learn from Waller, the British very smartly moved a beautiful young woman into Davis's apartment. She spent two nights there, and I think we may conclude that the little lady did not waste the British taxpayers' money all through that period of time. I would say that Bernard Davis must have by now been gotten into a frame of mind when he's ready to agree to the course of action that I indicated in my appreciation of June last.'

'You mean – we blew it, Joe?' grated the chairman. 'The British are all ready to tie up the deal of declaring the Davydovs as *de jure* rulers of the Ukraine?'

'Right!' affirmed Williams. 'But I think I see a satisfactory way out of the situation at this point of time.'

'Please, Joe!' wailed Steiner.

'I am proposing, Mr Chairman, that we in a sense pre-empt the findings of my appreciation of June last, and confound the British plot to use the Davydovs as a lever against the Soviets in next year's Worldwide Energy Convention . . .'

'Yes, Joe – yes?' breathed the chairman. And every eye was upon Williams, and every breath held in tension.

'. . . By presenting the Soviets with a copy of my appreciation of June last,' concluded Williams triumphantly. 'So that they can move in first and knock the hell out from under the goddam Limeys . . . *by themselves offering* de jure *rule of the Ukraine to the Davydovs!*'

By mid-afternoon, the tentative promise of an improvement in the weather had been coyly withdrawn, and that Monday the sixteenth relapsed into the familiar pattern of high winds and chilly rain.

Bernard sat by the telephone as the evening closed in upon Scunthorpe High Street, and the Christmas fairy lights came on in the shopping precinct, where the hardy Humbersiders, scorning umbrellas, strolled bare-headed under the drenching sky.

James had rung him shortly after three: he had found the Aston and its contents just where Bernard had left them on Saturday night, and all undisturbed. He was at the office with Alec, and they would both remain there and await developments.

The Russian rang again just after six . . .

'It is the well-wishers, Mr Davis. We have talked with our mutual friends and have been authorized to make you a very attractive offer.'

'That sounds fine,' said Bernard. 'Let's hear it.'

'That would not be discreet, Mr Davis. May we suggest that our spokesman rendezvous with you? Anywhere at your convenience.'

'Make it the offices of Fitch, Davis and Sons in Doncaster Road,' said Bernard crisply. 'The main door will be open. Tell your spokesman to come straight in at – ' he glanced at his watch – 'exactly seven o'clock.'

Without waiting for an acknowledgement, he put down the receiver and grinned at his reflection in the mirror.

The new Bernard Davis was quite going to his head! But, seriously, if only Father could see him now . . .

It was a short walk up to the offices, with the east wind at his back, shoving him along. He clutched the Biretta in his overcoat pocket, but estimated that there was little need of it. He wondered how Janice, that Maoist hockey-player, was making out in the cramped forepeak of James's boat; and had a sudden and stimulating remembrance of her sitting up in his bed in her shirt-waist or slip, on that famous occasion, before everything went black, and nothing had ever seemed quite the same since – a circumstance that he attributed to residual concussion and the slight headache that persisted. He supposed he had better see a doctor. But not now. Later, when the funeral was over and this business was safely concluded.

Crossing an intersection, he almost collided with a woman who came at him with head bowed against the wind and rain. He stepped aside, flashed her a grin – to which she responded with an eager smile. She was young and quite pretty. Nice.

He had telephoned ahead, and Alec and James were waiting for him in the partners' office that fronted the street, from which it tastefully hid itself behind net curtains gathered up with black satin bows. A portrait in oils of the late Edmund Fitch, by an Associate of the Royal Academy, looked gravely down from above the chimney-piece. On the chimney-piece, also, was a cunningly-wrought model of a coffin lying upon a bier, set under a glass dome.

'Well, our fellow will be here in just over half an hour,' said James, who appeared to be enjoying the situation. Alec looked terrible.

'Where's Garbisian now?' asked Bernard.

'In one of the locked drawers in the mortuary,' said James. 'Next drawer to the one where I put the reliquary.'

'You got him out of the Aston without any difficulty – the rigor mortis had passed off?'

'Yes, we found the corpse nice and supple, didn't we, Alec?' said James. He took something from his pocket and laid it on the desk before him: an upper plate of false teeth; very pink and very white, with a wink of gold here and there. 'These fell out of his mouth when we were carrying him in. It's pretty obvious they got lodged in his throat, and that's what killed him.'

'Of course,' said Bernard. 'That would account for it. There must have been some sort of scuffle. The poor chap half-swallowed his dentures and choked to death. What a rotten way to go. You're quite sure he wasn't also shot, or anything?'

'There isn't a mark on the corpse,' said Alec, adding with a touch of professional pride: 'We laid him out properly, in one of the lawn shirt-shrouds, the same as Father's wearing.'

'Alec's worried about tomorrow's ceremony,' said James.

'I had arranged a very quiet interment,' said Alec. 'No church service; just a modest affair in the cemetery chapel, with only family. Now see what happens – ' he brushed a sheaf of notes that lay on his blotting-pad – 'the phone's been going all day. Everyone wants to come: the Chamber of Commerce are sending a representative, and the local chapter of the Worshipful Company of Funeral Directors; the Humberside County Council, the Buffaloes, the Rotarians, the Lions. Our quiet funeral is going to end up looking like a state funeral!'

James gave a delicate cough. 'It's worse than that, you know. I'm afraid it's all over Humberside about Kitty's – I mean Ekaterina's – appearance at the cinema. The grapevine's filled in the bald details from the press. I'm afraid we're also going to have to put up with a horde of gawping rubberneckers.'

'Oh, my God!' cried Alec, burying his face in his hands. 'What have I done to deserve this?'

Poor old Alec, thought Bernard. But he doesn't know how very much worse it could have been. At least Father's going to be put away with his dignity intact – which is certainly more than the old devil deserved. Let's face it, our old man was nothing more than a common thief – and a murdering thief at that; though the extenuating circumstances of the civil war probably went some way to mitigate the stark awfulness of the killings.

Bernard was still musing on this – and his brothers were sunk in their own, private meditations – when the bell of the outer door went ting, and a tall figure showed behind the opaque glass doors of the partners' office.

James opened the door to the Russian spokesman, whom Bernard docketed as one or another of the ubiquitous characters in rubberized mackintoshes and wide-brimmed hats. The fellow looked so much like the stylized goblin figure of a Russian Bolshevik on which three generations of Davises had been reared, or were in the process of being reared, that one could scarcely take him seriously; why, he only needed a beard and a smouldering black sphere labelled 'Bombski'!

'Mr Davis,' the newcomer said to Bernard, 'I regret that our ensuing conversation must be confidential.'

Alec and James looked to their younger brother for a lead. He nodded to them, and they went out, shutting the office door behind them.

'Right,' said Bernard. 'Let's have your masters' very attractive offer.'

'You proceed hastily, as is your characteristic, Mr Davis,' replied the other. He had a long, pale face and pale eyes fringed with flaxen lashes that gave him a goat-like appearance. Bernard now knew him to be the one who had twice telephoned him.

'You don't have a lot of time,' replied Bernard. 'The Gregory reliquary is already under offer to the Chinese. All you have to do is better their offer, but I don't have all night.'

'First,' said the other, 'as to our conditions of trade.

We shall require the reliquary and its contents intact, to be placed into our hands. Alternatively, I am to be a witness to its total destruction. Either of these two conditions will satisfy.'

'No problem,' said Bernard. 'And what are you offering in return?'

'The Hetmanate of the Ukraine!' declared the Russian portentously. 'Hereditary *de jure* rule of the second largest republic of the USSR, for the head of the Davydov family and his successors!'

Only, it could not be the eldest son, Alec. The Bolshevik produced a copy of the evening paper from the capacious pocket of his rubberized mackintosh: a much-thumbed copy, whose front page headlines revealed as much of Kitty's aberration in the cinema as the ethics of journalism permitted – which was quite a lot.

Oh dear me, no. Thin-lipped with puritanical disapproval, Bernard's visitor gave him to understand that the dignity of the Union of Socialist Soviet Republics – not to mention the dignity of Soviet womanhood – could have no truck with that sort of goings-on. Kitty's mental breakdown was of a kind which forty-odd million Ukranians could not be expected to ignore. By a cruel irony, poor Kitty's ardour for the life aristocratic had deprived her of her heart's dream.

'The Hetmanate is offered to yourself, Mr Davis,' said the Bolshevik, 'or to your other brother.'

'Count me out,' said Bernard hastily. 'Let James have it. It will suit him well, and Maureen and the kids. But what exactly does the job call for? I mean, the concept of a hereditary ruler is a bit at variance with the canon of Marxist-Leninism as I understand it. Will old James and his missus and kids be expected to launch ships, open bridges, sit through interminable banquets listening to screaming old bores, accept bouquets from snotty-nosed tots – like some ruling families I could mention?'

The Bolshevik looked at him, goat-like and affronted. 'Indeed no!' he cried. 'For what other reason did we fight a Civil War and a Patriotic War, but to establish such privileges for the heroes of the State, to enjoy after lifetimes of service and dedication, of sweat and sacrifice – and never on the hereditary principle? All that will be required of the Hetman and his family will be a total retirement from public life and a sober consciousness of the dignity and splendour of the Soviet peoples!'

'You mean,' cried Bernard, 'that you're going to imprison them all in Lubianka gaol?'

The other snorted angrily. 'Not so!' he cried. 'The Hetman and his family will reside in circumstances consistent with the dignity and splendour of the Soviet peoples. Outside the borders of the USSR. In some neutral country. Preferably Switzerland.'

'I think,' said Bernard, 'that that will suit them a treat.'

'The rest of you,' said the Bolshevik carelessly, 'will be paid generous emoluments consistent with the dignity of the Hetmanate. In return, you will be expected to conduct yourselves with probity and decorum – and especially you will be expected to make sure that Mrs Kitty Davis so composes herself in future. Is it agreed, Mr Davis?'

'You're on!' cried Bernard. 'I will keep my part of the bargain, relating to the Gregory reliquary, immediately after my father's funeral tomorrow.'

'Ah! The former Excellency Prince Davydov,' said the Bolshevik. 'We have been instructed to procure a wreath to be laid on the *boyar*'s grave. From the Party Presidium – anonymously, of course.'

Bernard inclined his head in gracious thanks, and then an idea came to him . . .

'Tell me,' he said. 'Would your masters make this – if I may say so – bold and imaginative offer of the Hetmanate if my father had not been a former prince of the aristocracy?'

The other made a deprecating gesture and smiled. 'But that is purely hypothetical, Mr Davis,' he said. 'It is without doubt that your late father was – what he was.'

'But,' persisted Bernard, 'supposing he had been shown to be an impostor and not a *boyar* at all? Let us say, for the sake of argument, that he had been a starving deserter from the Bolshevik army, a frightened peasant lad on the run. Would the offer then have been made?'

The goat fact took on its affronted expression again.

'Indeed not, Mr Davis,' he cried. 'The Hetmanate would not be offered to just any riff-raff! What sort of people do you think we are?'

CHAPTER XI

The morning of the Davis funeral – long to be remembered in Scunthorpe – began with leaden skies, adumbrating yet another wet and windy day. The patriarch's new-dug grave had been given a substantial brick lining and, though covered by a tarpaulin, had an inch of rainwater at the bottom by ten o'clock.

At nine o'clock Bernard dressed himself in morning suit, black tie and top hat, and awaited the arrival of the firm's limousine that was to take him to his appointment with the Chinese faction. He was surprised by a ring on the door bell, and was even more surprised to find Mr Chuck Waller, the spy of the Americans, standing on his doorstep. Cowboy Waller's distant blue eyes were glazed with alcohol, his breath must surely have been a potential fire hazard – and all this at nine o'clock on a wet Tuesday morning in December.

'Mr Davis, sir,' he said. 'You wanna let me in? I got things to say to you. Apologies to make. Yes sir!'

'I've got to leave in five minutes,' said Bernard. 'But come in by all means.'

The man was soaked through, and brought a series of water pools through the flat with every squelching step. Bernard thought to offer him a drink – but decided not.

'I'm leaving,' said Waller. 'Off to South Africa. They know how to treat a white man in South Africa. Yes sir. Before I left, I had to say I was sorry for all the trouble I caused you.'

'That's all right,' said Bernard. 'It's practically all over now.'

'That I know,' said Waller. 'They told me to lay off, last night. But I'd already written out my resignation. It's South Africa for me. They respect a white man down there. Hey! Would you believe the way old Garbisian and me fooled them fat cats in Washington? Ha! We sure blew you folks up out of nothing and piled up the expenses. Poor old Garbisian. He was a white man, Mr Davis. You know that? You know all he ever wannad to do?'

'No. Tell me,' said Bernard, with a glance out of the window to check if the limousine had arrived.

Mr Chuck Waller closed his far-away eyes. When he opened them again, a broad grin split his rubbery face.

'That dame,' he said. 'That British broad that you had in here nights. Plenny style. Plenny class. And you know what? That dame downstairs. That Monica. She's got plenny going for her too. And you know what?'

'What?'

'She's crazy about you, Mr Davis. Man, I'm telling you no lie. Crazy about you.'

'That's nice,' smiled Bernard. 'Now, if you don't mind, Mr Waller, I've got to . . .'

'Hey!' exclaimed Waller. 'Did I ever tell you about poor old Garbisian and all he ever wannad to do? So I'm telling you. All he ever wannad to do was to be a United States citizen. Yes sir. He said to me. Christ, he said to me a million times. He said: "Chuck, all I wanna do is to die in the land that bore and nourished Thomas Jefferson." Ain't that nice? All he ever wannad to do was to die in the land that bore and nourished Thomas Jefferson.'

Mr Chuck Waller began to cry. Remembering Garbisian, Bernard suddenly felt a tightening of his own throat.

'He was a nice chap, Garbisian,' said Bernard.

'He was a beautiful guy!' cried the other. 'Bee-yoootiful!' And he sobbed brokenly.

A light was breaking in a dark corner of Bernard's mind. It opened like a sunburst and flooded his consciousness.

'Don't take on so, Mr Waller,' he said, laying a hand on the other's broad, bony shoulder. 'I've got the most wonderful idea. Listen – here's what you must do . . .'

Bernard's limousine drew into the yard at the end of the cul-de-sac at exactly nine-thirteen. Alec was waiting there – morning-suited and top-hatted also – with Father's heavy gold half-hunter watch in his hand and a wild look in his eye.

'Go straight into the workshop and get yourself a cup of tea, Thomas,' he ordered the chauffeur, in a tone which brooked no argument. The man departed.

Alec, who had worked out the time schedule for the Chinese operation, had arranged it so that none of the Fitch, Davis & Sons employees would be in or around the yard during the estimated, fateful five minutes of the evolution.

'How's your wife?' Bernard remembered to ask.

Alec's face softened. 'I went to see Ekaterina last evening,' he said. 'With the children. She didn't recognize me and the children, of course. She was very regal. Very fine.'

'Alec,' said Bernard, 'Alec, old chap, I'm terribly sorry about the way everything turned out for you. I know how much it must mean to you to be passed over by James. I know how much it would have meant for Kitty – Ekaterina – to be the wife of the Hetman of the Ukraine.'

'It's true, Bernard. Very true,' said his brother with a sad smile. 'But poor Ekaterina could scarcely know greater happiness than she knows now. For you see, Bernard, in her own mind, she's more than the wife of the ruler of the Ukraine – she's the Tsarina of all the Russias, the true incarnation of Catherine the Great!'

It was then that the Cathay Flower delivery van drove into the yard. Out piled the four grinning Chinese, and the biggest of them held out his hand to Bernard.

'Oh yes, Mr Davis,' he said. 'Hope I see you in the pink this morning.'

'I'm very well, thank you,' said Bernard. 'Did Miss Janice give you any idea of the size of the thing you've to pick up?'

'Oh no, Mr Davis,' grinned the other. 'Miss Janice did not inform us of that.'

'It's pretty bulky,' said Bernard. 'And it weighs . . . about two hundred and twenty pounds. It's also an awkward shape. For convenience sake, we've put it in a coffin. How does that strike you?'

'That's all right, Mr Davis.' The other spread his hands and widened his grin. Coffin or coke oven — it was all the same to the cheerful Chinese of the Cathay Flower, for whom Marxist-Leninism was one big laugh round the clock.

Dead on cue, Alec and James came out of the mortuary, wheeling a plain deal coffin on a trolley. The Chinese spat on their hands, took hold of the gunmetal handles and hoisted the coffin on to their massive shoulders.

'I take it you've had your orders about — er — forwarding the goods,' said Bernard. 'Miss Janice didn't give me any message about that.'

'Oh yes, Mr Davis,' said the spokesman, as they trundled the coffin into the back of the van and shut the door. 'All fixed, what we do with it. You bet. Straight to Leeds airport. Chop-chop.'

Bernard watched them go, taking off his topper as he did so. The wind brought a tear to the corner of his eye. He looked away and blinked.

'Now what?' demanded James the Hetman.

'Time to start for Vicarage Gardens,' said Alec, consulting his schedule. 'Bits and pieces department: the Polaroid camera and left-hand black leather glove are in your car, Bernard (what in the blazes do you want with a left-hand black leather glove? – forget I asked that); the you-know-what travels with me. James goes straight to the cemetery. Anything we've forgotten?'

Bernard scribbled in his notebook, tore out the page and gave it to James.

'Ring this Scunthorpe number right away, James,' he said. 'Speak only to a chap called Chuck Waller. Tell him that the goods are going straight to Leeds airport.'

'Right-o, Bernard.'

The five minutes tea-break was over; the men came strolling out of the workshop, straightening their faces and shutting off their light-hearted badinage. Practised masks of gravity were assumed; voices were hushed. Even such a banality as 'where's me flippin' ignition key', when delivered out of the corner of a turned-down mouth, and with a dying fall, can carry certain overtones of immortality.

Beneath the long, flat bonnets of the hearse and the three funeral cars, slow-turning engines purred discreetly. All eyes were upon Alec. As officiating director, he nodded to the chauffeur of the hearse, who let out his clutch and allowed the black and crystal vehicle to whisper forward; on, and out of the gates, the others following.

In this manner – the as yet empty hearse leading, and three matched limousines behind – they came at length to the house in Vicarage Gardens, where the late, false Prince Ilich Davydov lay awaiting them in his *chapelle ardente*, with his servant and occasional mistress kneeling in tears at the foot of the open coffin.

In fact, Minna Hodge was a thoroughgoing nuisance – as might have been predicted – and nearly ruined everything. She insisted that she would remain with her dead master, in the *chapelle ardente*, till the lid of the coffin was put on and screwed down. Nor was she to be dismissed with suggestions that she should fetch drinks for the brothers, and even have one herself. Finally, at a signal from Bernard, Alec started driving home the screws. It was then, and only then, that the woman fled from the room with loud sobs and went downstairs to take her place with Alec's family in the leading limousine, where all the neighbours could see and envy her.

Alec undid the screws again and took off the lid. What had to be done took only a few moments. Then they called in the pallbearers, who had been waiting out on the landing.

A fair-sized gaggle of people at the end of Vicarage Gardens (they were casual passers-by who had been attracted by the sight of the funeral cars and had put two and two together) provided the first intimation that the patriarch's interment was going to be something out of the ordinary. As the hearse and following limousines turned into the main road, a score of regarding faces were pressed to the windows, and many fingers were pointed at Minna Hodge. She, suspended between grief and gratification, could scarcely be expected to know that she was being mistaken for the daughter-in-law who had been so sensationally reported in the press. The rumour had passed around the town that Mrs Alec Davis would be attending the funeral in order to keep up family appearances – but that she would be wearing a straitjacket under her fur coat. A fur coat was expressly mentioned in all the versions, and it was this related detail which gave the rumour the tangy flavour of authenticity. Minna Hodge was wearing an old black-dyed coney.

The drive to the cemetery took the cortège past the Civic Centre, and it was here that other vehicles, containing representative mourners from many local institutions, moved out and joined the tail of the funeral cars. Alone in the last limousine, Bernard looked back and saw a police car coming to take up a shepherding station on his starboard beam. The officer in the passenger seat nodded and waved to him, and he experienced a distant physical shock on recognizing that his escorts were none other than Arnold and Ron.

A twinge of guilt, immediately quenched, was replaced by the comforting thought that – no matter what – he could never actually be accused of the murder of Garbisian, since the Armenian had manifestly died more or less accidentally. What was the jargon? – Death by Misadventure, that was it. Furthermore, in a very short while (he glanced at his watch), Garbisian's remains would be safely interred. He smiled across at Arnold and Ron.

They came to Cemetery Road, and saw the crowds lining the graveyard railings and sports ground opposite, where a dramatic line of poplars shivered nakedly against the sky. More faces pressed forward to peer, as the slow procession of cars went in between the iron gates and up the path that led to the miniature funerary chapel in the Victorian Gothic style, with tiny pointed windows and a bijou spire. The people were crowding the sides of the path, spilling on to the grass and standing upon the graves. There were police with walkie-talkies holding them in check.

Bernard got out and assisted Maureen and her children to alight from the limousine ahead of him. He saw the Bolsheviks standing in line by the door of the chapel: they looked like an execution squad. Their spokesman was scowling at him; to Bernard's alarm, he made a brusque gesture of summons. Bernard went over.

'Mr Davis,' said the man, 'you have deceived us. You have wilfully suppressed information from us!'

Bernard had had nothing for breakfast but a cup of coffee; he felt it churn in his stomach, and the man's long, pale face wavered in his vision.

He fought for something to say. 'I – I'm sorry,' he faltered. There did not seem much else to say. The whole thing had fallen apart. He supposed it was only the presence of the police and the watching crowds that restrained the Bolsheviks from drawing their pistols and performing a mass execution of the Davis family there and then. But where, he wondered, had he gone wrong? How had they got on to his game?

'You must have appreciated, Mr Davis,' said the goat-man, 'that the Soviet Union could not accept any *irregularity* in the relationships of the family that represents the Soviet peoples. The position must be regularized, or the whole proposition is null and void.'

'I'm afraid I don't . . .' began Bernard, bemused.

'The position of the child Sydney,' said the Bolshevik. 'The infant offspring of the girl Natasha. We cannot accept the illegitimate status of the child Sydney.'

'Little Sydney?' cried Bernard, relief giving way to indignation. 'But, man, this is nineteen seventy-four, coming on five. This is the permissive society. We've thrown off the turgid shibboleths of bourgeois morality in the West, and, in that sense, we've become more like you. It doesn't matter all that much here, any longer, that poor little chaps like Sydney came into the world without benefit of clergy.'

'It matters to *us*!' said the Bolshevik. 'Sydney will not do for the Soviet Union. We cannot allow the dignity of the Soviet peoples to be represented – even only on a *de jure* basis – by a family that carries the taint of illegitimacy. Something will have to be done about Sydney.' And the cold, goat's eyes narrowed dangerously.

'Good God!' cried Bernard. 'You surely don't mean . . . not little Sydney! I knew you chaps were pretty ruthless, but you surely . . .'

The Bolshevik silenced him with a gesture.

'Liquidation is not called for,' he said, 'if we are able to regularize the child's status. Is the girl Natasha aware of the identity of the father?'

'Of course she is,' snapped Bernard. 'What sort of girl do you take my niece for? Yes, she knows who he is. In fact, she's currently trying to slap a paternity order on him, but he's a bit evasive, being a sailor.'

'His name – and whereabouts?'

'You'd better ask Natasha herself,' said Bernard. 'There she is. Natasha, dear, would you come and have a word with this gentleman before you go into the chapel, please?'

Leaving them, Bernard stepped into the tiny chapel that smelt of flowers and was packed with the Davis family and their supporters. The coffin stood on a trestle before the plain wooden altar, and somebody – presumably Alec at the behest of Kitty before she went completely dotty – had provided an Imperial Russian flag to cover it.

The service began.

It was about this time that the Cathay Flower delivery van, travelling in a north-westerly direction along the A645 and heading for the Leeds Bradford airport, was waved to a halt by the driver of a truck that appeared to have skidded broadside across the road. The occupants of the truck – crew-cut and brawny young men in plain denims – fell upon the Chinese Take-Away *restaurateurs* and overpowered them by the firm application of superior numbers.

Leaving the four Chinese bound and gagged in the back of their parked van, the hi-jackers drove off with the coffin. By the time the obsequies of the late false Prince Davydov were drawing to a close, the selfsame coffin – still unopened, as had been instructed – was being loaded into a Boeing B-52 that was waiting for take-off to Washington.

The person who had set this operation in train – the newly-resigned Mr Chuck Waller – had already bought his ticket for South Africa. He was laughing.

The patriarch was lowered into his brick-lined and waterlogged grave, Tsarist flag and all, while his family stood round the hole, and the Bolsheviks formed a tight phalanx behind Bernard. The watching crowds – those uninstructed in the physiognomy of the Davises – were speculating on which of the mourning womenfolk was the nude madonna of Sunday's sex film show; opinions were fairly evenly divided between Alec's eldest daughter Olga and James's wife Maureen, with coney-coated Minna Hodge as a rank outsider.

It was teeming with rain, and the first rattle of earth on the coffin lid brought about the early break-up of the less committed members of the onlookers. Five stalwart gravediggers, specially commissioned by Alec, stepped forward, spat on their hands, and commenced to fill in the hole. Simultaneously – and with a lot of 'left hand down' and 'right hand down' and 'mind your backs, please' – a low-level loader crawled into the cemetery behind a plodding tractor. After it came a motorized crane; and resting upon the loader was the largest piece of funerary sculpture that Scunthorpe had seen in many a long day: a Victorian representation of a mourning angel with a dead baby across its knees, twice life-sized, in Carrara marble. Wholly unsuitable to place over the grave of a septuagenarian though it might have been, the giant angel and the baby possessed certain definite advantages: James it was who had telephoned round the masons' yards of the Humberside area for the most massive piece available for immediate delivery, regardless of cost.

While the gravediggers reduced the pile of earth, the graven block of marble was raised skywards on the end of the crane. Bernard held his breath and glanced across at the Bolsheviks, who were watching – like everyone else – with tremendous interest.

The instant the last shovelful of earth was thrown, a signal from Alec brought the sculptured mass down upon its firm brick base. And the last resting-place of the patriarch was sealed. Bernard exhaled his bated breath and sagged with total relief. He grinned wearily at his brothers. They gave him looks of ungrudging admiration – for had he not planned everything?

Now, people were coming up to the brothers, shaking them by the hand. The two young policemen approached Bernard shyly. An idea came to him.

'You'll remember,' he said, 'that I promised I'd tell

you if I recalled anything else about Garbisian? Well, I remember him saying that his greatest ambition was to emigrate to America. Presumably illegally.'

'Could be important,' said Ron. 'We'll pass that on, Mr Davis. That could be why he left his luggage behind – to put everybody off the scent. He's probably smuggled himself to America.'

Monica was there. Wearing a black coat and hat and coming towards him, shyly holding out her hand.

'Won't take up any more of your time, Mr Davis,' said Ron. 'Just wanted to offer deepest sympathy.'

'Wish you a long life,' said Arnold.

Monica's hand was very small and soft; the touch of it left him feeling strangely tender and protective towards her.

'Nice of you to come,' he said, 'in this dreadful weather.'

'I took a taxi,' she said.

'Look,' said Bernard. 'I can give you a lift back. Go and sit in the funeral car over there. I'll be finished what I have to do in a few minutes.'

'All right,' said Monica. 'Thanks ever so much.'

He watched her go. Goat-eyes was at his elbow when he turned back to the grave.

'Now we are ready to do business, Mr Davis,' said the Russian. 'And may we offer congratulations on a most touching and well-conducted ceremony? The question of the child Sydney, I would add, is already in hand, and we anticipate a speedy and satisfactory conclusion. Nothing remains but for you to hand over the reliquary.'

It was a divinely poignant moment, and Bernard drew it out for as long as he was able, savouring its charm. Then he pointed to the graven marble colossus.

'I can't,' he said simply. 'We've just buried it under all that, with Father.'

Bernard's triumph of organization had even included the detail of a flask of brandy for just such a contingency. They helped the stricken Bolshevik into one of the limousines and slipped a few sips between his pallid lips. Presently, the goat-eyes opened, alighted upon Bernard sitting opposite, and clouded over with pain and terror.

'It – it is not true?' he cried.

'It's true, all right,' said Bernard cheerfully. 'You blew it! While you were watching the birdie, the conjuror was slipping a rabbit into his sleeve. That reliquary is six feet under, and there it stays, in a perpetual interment.'

'We will have it raised!' wailed the Bolshevik.

'No one in the country, save the Home Secretary, can authorize the exhumation of that coffin,' said Bernard. 'And he won't do it at your behest. If your people wanted to take it by force, they'd have to raid and occupy a large chunk of Eastern England to do it; the size of that marble monstrosity precludes any sort of quick snatch-and-grab job. It's as safe there as it would be in the Bank of England – or within the walls of the Kremlin.'

'Why did you do this to me?' cried Goat-eyes.

'It's an insurance policy,' said Bernard. 'While ever that reliquary remains safely hidden away in Scunthorpe, your people are going to look after the Davises. You didn't really think I was going to hand it over, or let you destroy it, did you?'

The goat-eyes were haunted with dread. 'How are – they – going to believe me when I tell them?' he demanded. 'I was supposed to witness its destruction.'

Bernard smiled. From his pocket, he took a coloured photographic print and passed it to the Bolshevik. It had been taken with a Polaroid camera, by flashlight, in the *chapelle ardente* at the family home in Vicarage Gardens that morning. It showed the open coffin of the late, false Prince Davydov, with the patriarch lying in his long sleep – and with the Gregory reliquary nestling in the capacious coffin alongside him. One white hand lay across the bauble of gem-studded filigree; the other – masked with a black leather glove – was held stiffly to the side.

'We buried the prince with his prosthetic arm,' explained Bernard. 'The one he wore all the time he was in England.'

'Very tasteful, I am sure,' said the Bolshevik flatly.

'Now all you have to do,' said Bernard, 'is to tell your masters that *you* took the photograph and accompanied the coffin from there to its grave. I'm sure we can rely on your smooth tongue to put us *all* in the clear!'

After a while, and a little more brandy, the Bolshevik opined that this was probably so. By this time, the mourners had all gone, and the rubberneckers had drifted away. Under the dripping skies of Humberside, the angel colossus kept lonely vigil over the dead baby. Bernard went to join Monica in the other limousine.

The funeral in Scunthorpe was over.

CHAPTER XII

Monica's soft perfume permeated the limousine's interior. She was all softness, Bernard decided; and what he had put down to coquetry was really no more than a gentle desire to please him. He glanced indulgently at her hand – plump, pink and ungloved – that rested on the seat beside him. She really was an extraordinarily nice girl.

He looked up, met her fluttering gaze, and smiled encouragingly.

'I had a few words with your boy-friend Mr Waller this morning,' he informed her, 'and he told me he was going abroad.'

'To South Africa,' she said. 'And he wasn't really a boy-friend. More like an older brother. I shall miss him very much.'

A row of houses and scurrying, umbrella-bearing figures showed through the streaming windows. Very properly, the chauffeur was returning from the cemetery at only a slightly speeded-up funeral crawl. There was plenty of time before they reached the High Street.

Yes, she really was a very nice girl, thought Bernard. Strange how it had never occurred to him before that she was also very shy. Needed a bit of encouragement, to bring her out. He remembered Cowboy Waller's pronouncement about her feelings for him, Bernard. Looking back on their fragmented relationship, he decided he wouldn't be at all surprised if she was quite smitten on him.

'Now that my father's dead,' he told her, 'my middle

brother James is going to take up an appointment under the Soviet government. In Switzerland.'

'Switzerland must be very nice,' she said. 'All those lakes and mountains. I suppose you'll be moving into the house in Vicarage Gardens, Mr Davis?'

'Please call me Bernard,' he said. 'Please do – Monica.'

'I'm afraid my name isn't Monica,' she told him. 'That's my professional, business name. I'm really Doris.'

'I like the name Doris,' said Bernard. 'I haven't thought about the question of moving. We'll have to do something about Father's house, and I don't suppose my brother Alec will want it, because he's got a very nice place of his own. As for me – the flat's quite adequate for my needs. For me and my poetry-writing.'

She moistened her candy-pink lips, and her bosom rose and fell tremulously. 'Oh, Bernard,' she cried. 'Don't tell me you write poetry. How lovely. Do recite something for me. Something of your own.'

'Pleasure,' said Bernard. 'This is something that I've been working on for the last few weeks. And, do you know, the closing line's only just come to me. Here goes . . .

'Distant yet omnipresent music of airy flutes,
Wispy faerie imaginings,
Borne on these wondrous, elf-lit
Blue and gold-hued,
Mystic wonder-woodlands.'

'Oh, that was lovely!' cried Doris. 'Really lovely. You know, Bernard, I do oil painting. Yes, I'm enrolled at an evening class at the Tech. It's so – so – *comforting* to have an artistic hobby. Don't you find it so with your poetry?'

'My poetry – my *hobby*?' murmured Bernard, with the

scales falling from his eyes. 'Well, yes. I suppose I do find it a comfort. But I've never thought of it in that way before.'

The dying day of Tuesday 17th December brought many surprises to quite a few people. To James, going back to his boat at dusk, to free the prisoner in the forepeak, came the surprise that the enterprising Janice had apparently found some sharp instrument among the sails and cordage and had – at the expenditure of some time and energy, and only quite recently – freed herself by gouging away the lock. And, on the bulkhead in the main cabin, in a suitably scarlet lipstick, she had left a message, which he could only suppose to have some special significance for Bernard . . .

'On a blank sheet of paper, free of any mark,
the freshest and most beautiful characters
can be written.' – Mao Tse-Tung

Five hours in advance of Scunthorpe, Williams and his aides (but not the too-thrusting Jackson, who had opted for a diplomatic nervous breakdown and had taken a month's furlough) waited for the arrival of the important, but unnamed, object that Chuck Waller had claimed in a signal to have snatched from under the very noses of both the Soviets and the Red Chinese. Its arrival, in a cheap deal coffin with gun-metal handles, was something of a surprise. More surprising still – and infinitely horrific – was the sight of Aram Garbisian's staring, cyanosed face when they opened the lid.

The Armenian hedonist had reached, at last, the land of his dearest aspiration. With his arrival, the file on the Davydov Situation was closed. No one in the service of the United States had greatly benefited from the affair in the long run, and DeSoto, the only begetter whose **brain** child it was, least of all: that same morning, DeSoto was committed to trial on charges of tax fraud.

There were no surprises for Booters and Bimbo – both of whom had known all along that the whole thing would blow over during the long weekend, if left alone.

But surprises in plenty for a young deckhand of the Grimsby fishing fleet, whose trawler was intercepted and boarded by a Soviet destroyer that same afternoon. With scrupulous politeness, representations were made to the British trawler's skipper that the crewman in question was required ashore for compassionate reasons; and the skipper readily acquiesced to the arrangement. The destroyer conveyed the lad to Hull, where a marriage took place between him and Princess Natasha Davydov – and not entirely under duress.

The first week in February brought unseasonable sunshine and a false spring. Aconites showed thickly among the crematorium's landscaped lawns, and surely those were daffodils in bud beyond the screen of young cypresses. Down by one of the ornamental flower-beds, a gardener was emptying a container of ashes among the rose bushes, spilling the grey clouds down the fickle wind.

Bernard liked the crematorium. It lay in a quiet wood close by the athletic stadium (for good and practical reasons without doubt; the contrast, for contrast's sake, between physical achievement and physical dissolution was a piece of sophistry that surely would not have occurred to the civic fathers), with an easily-worked landscape after the manner of Forest Lawn – which is at the diametrically opposite end of the utilitarian scale from, say, Père Lachaise and Highgate cemeteries. Bernard thought the chapel very fine, also: a touch of the Frank Lloyd Wright and more than a hint of the Japanesque in the elegant roof.

A very civilized place to leave one's ashes. But each to his own, in death as in life. He supposed that James's bones would eventually rest in the chapel of that palace above Geneva, on which the Bolsheviks had taken a thousand-year lease (did they really think that the Davydov dynasty, or even Bolshevism itself, would last so long?). Aram Garbisian lay where his heart had longed to be. The old immigrant couple, who had recently moved into a semi-detached council house in the estate that overlooked the cemetery (they kept a round-the-clock vigil on the patriarch's grave, to make sure, on behalf of the Bolsheviks, that the colossus was never shifted), they would surely make their end in Scunthorpe.

The cortège purred to a halt near the chapel door. Bernard got out of the hearse and glided swiftly to the limousine that contained the principal mourners. Alec did the same at the other side. Bare-headed and hat in hand, both of them, just as Father had always demanded.

The brothers exchanged barely perceptible raisings of eyebrows – and opened the limousine's doors in unison. It was beautifully done.

Bernard Davis had found himself: he had been there all the time.